ALSO BY NEIL JORDAN

Night in Tunisia
The Dream of a Beast
Sunrise with Sea Monster
Shade
Mistaken

THE PAST

THE PAST

NEIL JORDAN

SOFT SKULL PRESS
AN IMPRINT OF COUNTERPOINT
BERKELEY

The Past
Copyright © Neil Jordan 1980
This edition published in 2012 by Soft Skull Press

Library of Congress Cataloging-in-Publication Data is available.
ISBN 978-1-59376-510-1

Cover design by Faceout Studio
Interior design by Megan Jones Design

Soft Skull Press
An imprint of COUNTERPOINT
1919 Fifth Street
Berkeley, CA 94710
www.softskull.com

Printed in the United States of America
Distributed by Publishers Group West

10 9 8 7 6 5 4 3 2 1

To my mother and father

ONE

CORNWALL, 1914

1

T WO POSTCARDS OF the holiday town in the south-west of
England. They show the same scene which makes me think
they were chosen thoughtlessly, bought together maybe in the same
shop without caring a whit what the picture showed. Or bought
separately, two months between them. She had forgotten, of course,
what the first one displayed by the time she came round to needing
the second. Both are yellow and with serrated edges, yellowest at the
edges as if singed by a match. But the flame is time and the smell, far
from the smell of burning, is the smell of years.

火

THEY DON'T SHOW the sea or the town, just the esplanade. But from
the look of it, even across years, one can't doubt that this row of
dowdy four-storey houses faced the sea. And from the look of them
too one can surmise a town behind this esplanade that lives off this
esplanade and all year waits for the time when the canvas awnings
are stretched out and the canvas deckchairs are placed in the front
porches. For the houses are obviously hotels and the angular porches
are so obviously looking at what in the brochures must have been a
sparkling blue sea, one can be sure that the esplanade was wide and

elegantly paved, that there were railings on which to lean and maybe even white iron chairs on which to sit and watch that sea, perpetually blue and be cooled by its salt breezes. And there were rows of primitive paddle-boats (they had them then?) rocking, listing on the edge of the tide, and along the strand itself a row of canvas bathing huts. Canvas! Yards and yards of it are implied, painted in those circus stripes, those warm blues, fawns and yellows, stretched over windbreakers, tautened umbrellas and Punch and Judy stands and even barrel-organs. Was it the age of canvas? For the esplanade is full, there must have been attractions galore with which to fill it—and a spa too, behind the town, backed on by the houses, with the heavy lead taps and the metal baths. Was it the age of spas? For of the people who fill the esplanade, immobile and thronging, the women are most obvious, carrying sun-umbrellas. Was there devotion to water, a suspicion of sunlight? In the postcards they look like white, straight brushstrokes, their umbrellas like brighter dabs. And behind each woman, in her shadow almost, is always the predatory form of a man. They arouse my jealousy these men, suspicious themselves of sunlight, at times each man could be each woman's shadow, so much in her shadow he is. But then the whole image is drenched in sunlight as if the shot had been over-exposed or the card bleached by its years on some green felt desk near a window, through which the sun shone. But despite the bleaching of years, the blaze of sunlight could only have come from the day itself, a hot 'salad' day, and there were more of them then for the handwritten date on the back is June the First 1914. The message scrawled underneath is peremptory, almost irrelevant. Back in two weeks, Una. This though she knew, she must have known, her stay would last more than seven months. Which brings us to the main fact the card can speak of, besides sunlight and years—that she was a compulsive liar. The second card bears the same scene, the women still encased in sunlight though the sky must have leadened in those seven months since season, even then, must have followed season. And the message too promises a two-week return. But the signature is different—Una, Michael, Rene—and behind that last name there is a coy mark of exclamation (!). Which brings us to the prime fact that this card proclaims—the birth of her child. And one third fact, perhaps subsidiary, proclaimed by the months that intervened—between the first card and the second the Archduke Ferdinand was shot in Sarajevo.

2

L ILI'S HOUSE RISES four storeys, like those hotels. Lili lives on the fourth. There's a door which I put my shoulder to, then a dim staircase. There's the smell of moist brickwork, of the canal outside. Memory, she told me once, is mother to the Muses. But what do I know of all those years, of Dev and the Clare election and the Custom House fire? The ashes rose over the city, she told me, of the burnt files of each birth, marriage and death. Then they fell like summer snow, for three days. Lili walked through them, maybe held out her palms, caught the down of her birth-cert on the rim of her schoolgirl bonnet. I would petition her for memories like these. I felt a sharp angle in the banister's curve. I saw the landing then, and Lili's room. I saw Lili, by far the oldest thing in that room. When I entered, she turned in her perpetual cane chair. She smiled.

⚘

'UNA WENT THERE,' she told me, 'to have the child you want to know all about. She went there because she was pregnant, had got married because she was pregnant, one of those sublime mistakes they made then as well as now. He did the dutiful thing, though I'm sure he loved her. I can't imagine him not loving anyone and by all

accounts she was a beauty then, not the blousy Republican I got to
know later. They married and chose that place for their honeymoon.
He was from a Redmondite family, a lawyer with that blend of innocence and relentless idealism that was admirable then, really admirable, and that took the Free State to sully it. He was the best of them,
by far the best of them, he was marked out for what would happen
to him later, I've heard that said, having no way of knowing, my
only memories of him are in the kindergarten school out near Mount
Merrion, he'd come to visit us in his Free State uniform, the darling of
the nuns with those glazed eyes that told you precisely how much he
hated it, the heavy ridiculous belts and the shoulder pistols, he must
have hated it even more than de Valera hated him, he would walk
through the classroom in his wide boots, stammer while refusing the
nuns' offer of tea and lift Rene on to his hip. I remember her crying
once, with joy at first, and then pain at the buckle of the belt against
her backside, his large hands lifting her higher to nuzzle against the
shoulder pistol. Then there would be a few words of affection that
only demonstrated how little they knew each other when there would
be a respectful knock on the school door, the shadow of an N.C.O.
outside, and he would have to leave. I learned later it had always
been like that, ever since she was old enough to know him, which is
the trouble with public men I suppose, especially the kind of public
men we had then. But those few brief meetings were enough to convince anyone of his innate goodness, the quiet enigma of him, which I
suppose she inherited. And you could see how marriage to Una, who
was supposed to be a beauty then, who was pregnant by him, would
have been natural to him, an extension of that undifferentiated love

with which I imagine he first made her pregnant. But then I could be wrong, we could be all be wrong.

'All I can really tell you is that they went there, that she was pregnant when they went there and that they stayed nine months. The war had broken out, which would have afforded him an excuse to stay. They would come back, a married couple with a child with a respectable if somewhat fine interval between ceremony and birth. And though I would lay such duplicity at her doorstep, he must have been party to it. The only point behind all this information being the fact that Rene was a love-child—'

3

S O I EXTEND the picture on the postcard beyond the serrated
edge with a line, say, of unobtrusive shrubs, not quite trees,
between the esplanade and the road proper. These shrubs are in
wooden boxes, bound by metal hoops, smaller than those ladies and
their parasols and so invisible in that miniature scene; yet stretching
down that esplanade far beyond the confines of the postcard to where
the esplanade must end, to where steps must run down to the strand
leading to a wharf, the upright stakes of which reflect in the water
beneath, the scene most perfect, most symmetrical when the water
is calm. These shrubs will grow, of course, into the palms I imagine
them to be with their aching stems and stunted foliage, redolent of
a more torrid climate since they are transplants, burgeoning their
way into later postcards, ones that I shall never see. Though they
stand now in their temperate soil and their hoop-bound boxes with
just their palms flapping in the breeze for their trunks are resistant.
Facing the esplanade, the wharf, the water. And behind them the road
proper, the line of houses. Not just that row of regular Edwardian
façades behind the postcard parasols, but a row differentiated into
houses and hotels. More hotels than houses, if the town is as I imagine it, and these hotels in turn differentiated into those which drew
attention to themselves and those which didn't. Among those which

didn't, one moderately anonymous, intimating solid comfort on a small budget. With a canvas awning like the others and a tiled porch, the walls on either side painted blue and cream, the windows white. The paint was three summers old perhaps, bubbling under the brick. And its name, Excelsior, painted of course in gold above the first row of windows, rich between the blue below, the cream above.

The palms flap and the water waits for them. They would have pronounced the name roundly, presuming its importance. The cabbie grunts, hearing it, knowing their status. Or would they have walked, unsure of cabbies, unsure of what to tip; Irish, intimidated by the parasols, carrying their cases, their clothes too heavy for the hot day and just the palms intimating a welcome, flapping in their still boxes, whispering the confidence that they too are transplants to this imperial soil.

火

'UNA WAS AN actress, of the worst kind, the kind that insists on you calling them by their first name. Oonagh, Oona, Una, I stumbled over it so much at first, I didn't want to be on first name terms, damn her, I was a girl of nine or ten and hardly knew her, Mrs O'Shaughnessy struck me as much much safer. I was a wily child you see, suspicious of this mother of my friend with her large blowsy kisses and her first names. Children read adults, don't they? An atrocious voice with a loud, melodramatic presence, Una never acted anyone but herself but she had the luck to be an Irish speaker and so to meet Messrs Yeats and Fay and then gradually to be thought of as the Irish woman resplendent, though her hair was mousy and her eyes pale and her face totally devoid of those high cheekbones that were meant to be typical of the Celt. Though she had plenty of Matthew Arnold's refusal to submit to the tyranny of fact, the fact being that her stage presence was embarrassing and her refusal to submit to this being quite remarkable and, in the end, a triumph. But then to be fair I only saw her later, years later, when her figure had bloomed and when Rene and me were ten or twelve. When she met him I myself was just a blush on my mother's cheek and Una O'Shaughnessy was by all accounts, sorry to repeat myself, quite a renowned beauty. But then those were the early days of the Gaelic League and as you know yourself a certain kind of passion and what they called "nobility" and in particular an ability to speak Irish, more particularly among those who couldn't, was regarded as an adequate substitute for beauty, not to mention talent. And the kind of acting she relished when her husband met her didn't take place in theatres on legitimate stages, no, nothing as vulgar as that, it found its place in drawing-rooms before select groups of thoughtful people who would gather to look at representations or friezes from their imaginary history of Ireland. You would have the "Rape of Drogheda", say, and after hours of fuss with everyone finally seated and the whispering behind the drawing-room curtain finally stilled the same curtain would draw back to reveal, if you can picture it, a few painted flats to represent Drogheda's walls and a group of ardent young Gaelic Leaguers dressed as Cromwell's Roundheads with whatever pikes and muskets they could drum up for the occasion, all standing to one side in a balletic group, pointing their pikes and things towards a group of just as ardent young girls who represented the Maidens of Drogheda. And between them both, dead-centre of course, raised on a platform, a dais, would stand Una O'Shaughnessy, who else, dressed as Kathleen in a coat of flowing green with a petticoat of red and a symbolic chain maybe round her wrists, her face contorted into an expression of frozen pain, horror or melancholy, whichever was most appropriate. They engrossed my mother's generation, those idiotic affairs. Una, by all accounts, made quite a name from it and it's quite probable, if probability is what you're looking for, that he met her there and that her Kathleen ni Houlihan began the liaison that would lead to Rene's birth in that English town you want me to talk about and which I can't, of course, having never been there. But these idiotic affairs died a death, of course, as soon as the quite amazing discovery was made that the Roundhead youths don't really have to remain like limestone statues but can actually move and fortify their expressions of hate with violent gestures. And from there it was only one step into words, blessed words. "O my dark Rosaleen, do not sigh, do not weep, the priests are on the ocean green . . ." And thus Una became an actress. But she could never play O'Casey, despite her lineage. And why not? Because O'Casey demanded more than a green costume and a *blas*, he was music-hall and melodrama, farce and real tragedy and only a real actress could have done it. And she knew this, of course, and when *The Plough* came on she shouted her guts out from the pits with the rest of them, even though Mr Yeats shouted his apotheosis from his private box. And I know, I know, all this is beside the point, but what do I know of her pregnancy and that English town except for the fact that the child inside her would partake in none of her faults and would be called Rene—'

*

So heartened by the flapping palms they would have walked under the canvas awning, Una's heels striking the tiles, dragging the tufts of carpet in the hallway with her and striking again the hard oak stairs; and into a clean bedroom, with the walls cream-white, the ceiling done in necklaces of plaster; with a bed which they would find to be warm, with a film of damp.

There must have been a table with an oval scoop for an enamel basin. And the table would hold an enamel jug. All three of them white, echoing the walls and the slight curve at the pit of the jug echoing her form. The guest-book below reading 'Michael and Una O'Shaughnessy' in a young, perhaps a bold hand.

4

'I DO KNOW THERE was a spa there. With those sulphur waters that she claimed gave Rene her complexion—'

☙

SO I EXTEND the rim of the postcard even more, down the esplanade, past the steps and the wooden pier, where the palms and hotels ended, where the watering-place was, with maybe a sulphur bath. And Michael O'Shaughnessy, as young and admirable as you said Lili, reading *The Times* in the oak-panelled lounge of the hotel room, the browns mixing finely with his light tweed suit, English in its cut, sitting only a little awkwardly on his frame, set against the strength of his cheekbones and the tousled mop of his hair. He is thinking of Redmond and Home Rule while the thin light on the oak panels slowly becomes a blaze. Later he will think of Arthur Griffith and conscription, later again of de Valera and parades. But always as an afterthought, to the sweeps of light on the oak panels as he rises and goes to the window and sees the sun and the sea making a flat mirror beneath it. And his wife meanwhile is on the promenade, for the time being without that fiery quality you saw in her, just pregnant now, her belly like a swollen pod proud before her, meeting the

Cornish breezes. Una hides nothing of her shape nor of the flush of her cheeks. Her dress is bulky and white and she walks like a billowing flag of a new nation down to the wrought-iron chairs to drink three cups of that mineral water and pray that it will bring the same flush to her daughter's cheeks. She prays quietly, watching the sea, hoping as everyone does for a magic child. She rises then, her stomach swollen more with the gaseous liquid and walks back, or if the breeze is too strong, takes a hansom cab to her husband who is still by the window, watching the same sea.

Because that was the first month and it would have still been a honeymoon month and the war hadn't yet broken out or the Parliamentary party been split and their bodies just might have made those shapes on the dampish bed like those maps in which the larger island envelops the smaller one, backwards admittedly, but expressive of an act of union rather than one of buggery or rape. The play of their bodies, warranted by that honeymoon under the ceiling with the plaster necklace would have been a gift to them, would have made their differences opaque. They would have lain, counting the plaster pearls which would have led, maybe, to a plaster dimpled Cupid in the centre, they would have kept smiling at its white penis and perhaps even made jokes. It would have taken two months for their differences to emerge, the repetitive whisper of an old word that slowly becomes a roar, for her swelling stomach to take its toll with its moods, its impatience with things physical, its ancient irrationality that he feels he has met before in different guises, perplexing to him at first, then deeply disturbing, a disturbance he would have kept private, however, that would merely have given to his mouth a tight, perplexed line. His face that later became a mask, unrevealing and yet somehow like glass, transparent and still hidden from her as it would later be to masses of others. And his eyes that don't want to speak for fear of what they might say would have risen further moods in her, loud silences and even louder words. For she has taken to sitting up late, Lili, smoking cigarettes, filling the enamel basin with them while he sleeps. And from sitting up late she rises even later. He leaves the bed and dresses under the plaster boy while she sleeps, each breath like the exhalation of centuries. And the flush of a month ago is rocked in that sleep so he dresses alone, dines alone and soon can't imagine things otherwise. And the later she sits up the later she rises until she is hardly awake for two hours of daylight. Is it the fear, he wonders, that as her stomach grows larger until even her billowing skirt can't hide it she might meet someone from home who will take back news of her advanced condition? A remote possibility, since they are now well past autumn and fine weather and the resort is empty but for the old, the invalid and the local. But he suspects it, hearing her talk of that 'bunch of jackals back home'. He asks her is she afraid of the prying eye, the rumour carried across water to that country where there is only rumour and everybody is related. But she hears this slur on her native country and her voice grows shrill in its defence, her nationalism growing with her belly. His is beginning to wane. He sees a war on at last, to end all wars. He travels to London to hear Redmond speak, meets friends of his student days in khaki, thinks of signing with the Irish Guards. From a bench in Hyde Park he hears an anti-Redmondite called Bulmer Hobson and the name reminds him of seabirds and kelp and he sees the flushed, hard faces he knew back home surrounded by the black plumage of the constabulary. He hears the words Home Rule used as a taunt

and the names McDonagh, Plunkett, Pearse and the words flutter like
fledglings in the wind around him, a renewed attempt at the age-old
flight. He spends the night in a boarding-house near St Pancras and
can't sleep on the damp mattress. He sits upright on a hard chair the
way he knows his wife is sitting, remembering the beat of those words
against the wind, they smacked of Parnell and separatist passion, of
the strident lyrics of Young Ireland, the dense labyrinths of Fenianism
and gradually the war drifts from his mind and with it the thoughts
of volunteering and his mind reverts to the fulcrum it has never really left. He sits through the night with the image of the hotel, the
sea and his wife's two hours of daylight, static, placid and somehow
irreparable. And when the day comes up again and he can see again
through the window the chaotic shapes of St Pancras he rises, takes
his case and leaves, having decided nothing, knowing there is no decision, what is is and what must be will be. And as he travels back he
thinks of history, sees something old, tarnished and achingly human
rising out of the chaos of the present with all the splendid, ancient
unpredictability of a new birth. He reaches the station and the last
guests from the hotel are waiting to leave by the train he has arrived
on. Only the perennial eccentrics are left now, Lili, and the summer
prostitutes. He walks the promenade and feels one with these eccentrics. He feels outside time, events pass round him, he is in another
time, an older time, his mind, once so energetic, so logical becomes
a glaze through which he sees the world scream on a distant, opaque
horizon. Only the tiles of the promenade have substance, and the
vertical supports of the pier, their shadows in the water. He repeats
the word 'soul', he feels his fabulous bicep and wonders is it real.
The sea falls away beneath him and the flapping palms and holds the

sky in reverse, and does it contain, he wonders, the proper order? He sits with Una until his eyes grow heavy, then sleeps before she does. Awake at nine, slipping out from beside her unmoving body, having breakfast in the lounge downstairs, he leaves orders for the same to be brought for her whenever she wakes. He stands by the window watching the sun change the oak from brown to tan, leafing through *The Times*, *Manchester Guardian* and *Telegraph*, reading every inch of the small print, the tiny ads, anything that would keep his mind from the main headlines. And then he walks, Lili, to the now empty sulphur baths and drinks a ritual glass. He has become superstitious about the yellowish liquid. He looks in its swirling for a shape or a sign, a hint of the future, for the whorls of their lovemaking, a map of a world, of the past few months that are changing perhaps not only his life. Then he walks back, a little hurried, afraid to give himself more than half an hour lest she has awoken. He finds her half-awake, then slipping into sleep again. So he walks again, returns again, talks with her sporadically until she wakes fully around seven, dresses and they go downstairs to dine.

⽕

'SHE HID HER pregnancy so well, you see, that no one noticed, my mother didn't anyway, I'm sure of that and Una must have blessed herself in thanks when the war to end all wars broke out, it could have happened for her benefit, it gave her nine months' grace. And what was more natural than that he, coming as he did from a good family of Home Rulers, Redmondite in the best sense my mother always said, what could have been more natural than that he would

think of enlisting and would spend months thinking about it? And
so she must have blessed the Archduke Ferdinand for getting himself
shot and the Kaiser Wilhelm for taking it to heart and the flower of
Britain's manhood for rallying to the cause of Life, Liberty and the
Rights of Small Nations. But there were rumours all the same. I heard
years later from people that hardly knew Rene at all that in fact she
wasn't her mother's child but was born of a liaison between her hero
of a father, dead years by then, and a south of England music-hall
artiste or some such figure and was being kept in trust. But take it
from me, that's all nonsense, she was born of Una in your postcard
paradise, she was her father's child.'

⚑

SOMETHING HAPPENS TO him. He loses his will and gains it. He
discovers that part of himself later to become the whole of himself,
the self of indomitable will, of odd humanity and gentleness that we
know, Lili, from the history books. His mind becomes glazed, he
interprets this as weakness. Certain thoughts obsess him, not in the
logical, forward manner in which he had been schooled, but they
recur eternally, come to no conclusion, seep through his perceptions
to disturb him and then vanish before he can order them. He thinks
of death and the soul, of a mystical order that seems to have begun
with him, that will end with him. He longs to resume his studies
again, the world of books, legislature and ordered reading, a long-
ing that he feels in his stomach at times like a knot of physical pain.
But the other element saps his will, seduces him. He orders books
from London and leaves the packets unopened behind the desk

downstairs. He wakes one night well past midnight and is unsure whether he is awake or dreaming because instead of sitting in her chair and smoking beside him she is asleep, her six-months' stomach curving upwards, her eyelids slightly open. Her eyes are like needles underneath the lids. He raises his head and stares at the slivers of light, barely revealed under her drawn lids, the source of which is somewhere beyond her dilating nostrils and her closed mouth. With each breath she takes her head moves slightly on the pillow and the lights move too until he stares at her, hypnotised by them and the rainbows round his own lashes. Her breath rises with the sadness of death and with each wave he is carried further from those points of her eyes until he is seeing them across aeons of distance, two barely visible specks of light. It is his own death he is swimming in and the feeling of unearthly ease, of buoyancy, lulls him like a massaging hand, irresistibly. He thinks, I can return or stay here. And his will expands then like a rearing horse, mighty, more than irresistible and bears him back. She is sleeping still, with her eyes now fully closed.

Meanwhile the winter is beginning, the dry cold wind from the Azores whipping spray along the promenade, dispersing hillocks and ripples of sand over the austere tiled pathway. He leaves her around twelve, ignoring the wind. The sun is shining independently of it and but for the cold biting into the cheekbones, eyelids and fingers one could imagine the promenade crowded with its quota of summer strollers. It is empty though, as if the weak sun shines only for him. He grips his overcoat tightly around him and imagines that he feels neither wind nor cold but that just what he sees is real—the bright sunshine, like a blessing, clear and even sharper than in heat, over the pier, the iron chairs, the strand and sea, the canvas whipping round the few remaining bathing shelters. He thinks sunshine and emptiness are his element and so familiar seems the scene that he almost misses the one obtrusive shape—the girl standing in the shadow the bathing hut throws towards the sea.

He saw her from behind and then she vanished, or seemed to. He walked by the tottering structure of painted canvas and saw her again, in a discoloured fawn coat, looking at the sea. From her stillness and her pose, the way her fawn coat merged with the sand and then her head and shoulders glowed against the lime-grey sea, he knew that she had seen him. He stopped and heard the silence of his absent footsteps against the tiles. He looked at the sea with her, its washing exhausted, spent. She was in the damp part of the sand and her boots were sunk. Her hands were in the pockets of her coat and there were threads hanging from them and round the calves of her boots the stitching was split. The canvas flapped, and the palm leaves. He knew that she would turn, that her face would not surprise him. She turned and looked at him. Her eyes were resentful and hopeless. They were blue. Could he have known at that distance or could the sea have suggested the colour to him? But then even the sea was lime-grey. He knows she is one of the last of the summer prostitutes, perhaps even the last. She looks as redundant as the bathing hut or the hotel signs. He decides immediately to give her money, if not warmth.

'They've all gone, have they?' His voice surprises him in the silence.

'Who've all gone?'

Her accent is local. Perhaps he has been wrong. He stumbles for words. 'The starlings.'

She is shifting her feet in the damp sand as if she wants it to flurry, to be dry, to call the summer back.

'That sand is damp. Come up.'

'No, you come down.' And a humorous flicker crosses her face. 'The gentleman always does.'

He must climb over the railings and leap. She smiles, waiting for it. Does she notice his honeymoon shoes, scuffed after months of walking, his tweed suit now shapeless round his knees? Has she seen him walking, his aimlessness not too different from hers? She must have. He jumps and sinks to his laces in the sand. She walks to him, faintly smiling, takes his arm and leads him down the beach without a word.

5

'Would Una have talked to him incessantly about the Hungarian policy and Arthur Griffith, about Sinn Fein and shoneenism, telling him that if he enlisted he was just as guilty as any Protestant on a horse? I don't think so. She would have embodied the nation aggrieved, reclining on the bed, pillows propped around her, every long dramatic pause saying more than any tirade could have; theatrical pose and political history were inseparable for her. He would be by the window, listening. I espied them both in that pose years later, in a different room. By then he was in uniform, a dull smoky khaki, the colour of gorse. Her colour. He showed no extraordinary intelligence, not in the normal sense anyway, while she had a fast, quick mind that always outdid itself. He would have let her words seep through him, like old wine through a muslin cloth which comes out slowly, but purely, all the sediment removed. So when he later took his part among the minor heroes, she could claim he was her creation, she could put the point of his conversion in that hotel of yours. There was more, she would tell us, than Rene being born—'

She shifted in her cane chair and smiled.

'Irish, now, there's what I mean, Una could half speak it, a ridiculous *blas* she had when I remember her, but by then maybe she had forgotten most of it. Her father being an early Gaelic Leaguer,

who knows she could even have gone to the school of the unruly
stammerer, what was it called, St Enda's, and read the motto daily, I
Care Not Though I Were to Live But One Day and One Night if Only
My Fame and My Deeds Live After Me. And he though he couldn't
speak a word then yet he knew it later, became dutifully impeccable,
sent dispatches in both languages on the back of cigarette packets and
devised a code in it which Eoin MacNeill even couldn't crack. Now
why? He didn't love her, couldn't have, later anyway from what I
remember of them, he saw her only on flying visits from his flying
column and maybe at Christmas, holy days. So why did he take those
parts of her, reproduce them so meticulously, make his own mirror of
them, graft them on to his own person so perfectly that when the end
came she could claim he was her creation? And if you want an answer
and if you want the music of things in their proper place all you can
look to is the story. She made those claims of hers in retrospect, when
he was already being embalmed in the oil and the scent of the great
losers, and she put the point of his conversion there, in that hotel of
yours. But then she was part of the story too, she was his entry to it,
both of them making it as they were telling and Rene being born—'

火

BUT MICHAEL HAS pulled his boots out of the sand and has walked
along the beach with the girl whose name, he discovers, is June. She
is an alert and a nervous talker, she reveals large tracts of herself to
him immediately and yet leaves him with the impression that beyond
these tracts it would be indelicate to probe. Her teeth are small, her
face is small, somewhat drawn, with large brown eyes and sallow

cheeks leading to a dimpled chin. Her face has none of the definition that would give it beauty but can in certain lights be beautiful, depending on its mood and pallor. When not beautiful it could best be described as drawn and he will find, in fact, that her face is in continual motion between one aspect and the other. They walk along the strand between the dunlins and oyster-catchers and they talk about their lives. She talks of her boarding house, not along the promenade like his hotel, but in the smaller streets where the promenade becomes a road and the line of the palms ends and the spa has not yet begun. She spills out tracts of herself as if to put him at ease, punctuated now and then by a light laugh and a dry cough. She has been six months in the town, she tells him, and her sojourn in it seems as disembodied as his. But she knows more about it, she mentions names and streets and places he has never heard of, and leaves him feeling even more foreign, only native to the palms, the promenade, the pier. She talks of the war and the sea and of what she calls her 'present state'. The phrase leaves him wondering about her past one and since her accent is good and her words are redolent of governesses, a somehow childish innocence with an adult pretension towards exactitude, he wonders whether before her 'present state' she was a teacher of some kind. He feels there is something Quaker about her, in the plainness of her clothes and her air of Protestant rigour. And yet walking beside him she is as disembodied as he, as will-less, and he is given the impression of limitless time waiting to be spent. An air of decided sensuality emanates from the fawn coat, from the body it covers, which seems a little forlorn, like a boat stranded and waiting for the tide it knows will come and seep round its hull. He walks with her, wondering could he carry his own needs as honestly as she does hers. He talks of the war, the sea, the town, of everything but those private areas of his life which he knows, glancing at her whimsical brown eyes, he must never touch. He laughs at one of his own expressions—having compared the jowls of a dead dogfish that lay across their path to those of Kitchener—and finds himself surprised at the person who made the observation and the person who subsequently laughed. He can see in himself a new and lighter personality emerging, which seems to be his own creation. He cocks his mental eye askance at it, walking down the strand. They come to the pier and climb up the steps. She peels bark from the stem of a palm, he rests on the wedge of the barrel. A cold gust of wind blows up and so they move into the foyer of an old hotel and then into the lounge. It is an even less respectable hotel than his and he wonders if he had come here months ago, would it all have been quite different. They drink a pot of steaming coffee. Then they leave and walk back along the strand, she insisting that they retrace their steps in the sand, placing her feet in the prints his have made the way a child does. There is silence between them now and this silence acts on them like an inevitable suggestion, leads them up to the flapping, gaudy canvas of the hut where she saw him first. She leads him inside with her Quaker matter-of-factness to the forefront. He sees there are deckchairs stacked against one canvas wall and a bundle of straw mats. She smooths one out on the sand and with practised hands, and barely lifting her skirt, she gives herself to him.

火

IT BECOMES HIS pattern, and not one that's to be measured in days or hours, but one that has its own rhythm. Every day he walks down the promenade and the sun is as clear as when he came there first, the sky as clear, the only difference being the gathering coldness of its light. And some days he meets her there, an average of one day out of four, but never with regularity. There would be three days in a row at times, and then not one day for a week. He comes to think of these days as 'the day' and every day he thinks, 'Today will be the day.' And yet on the days on which he doesn't meet her he is never disappointed and on the days on which he sees her from above the canvas bathing hut he is pleased but not surprised. He is coming to accept the arbitrary nature of events as if the events themselves are objects of fate, dictated by a rhythm of which he is not master but servant. He surrenders his will to the accidental with the certainty that the pattern it will reveal to him will be greater than any he can impose. He thinks of Bulmer Hobson in Hyde Park, of Lord Kitchener, the Archduke Ferdinand, and of his sleeping pregnant spouse, curled like an esker in the room he has left, and walking along the promenade, anticipating June's fawn coat behind the gaudy canvas, anticipating the texture of sand and of the bark of palms, anticipating the same canvas flapping emptily without her, he feels a remarkable freedom in his total acceptance of whatever chance dictates. And when she is there they will walk, repeat the first day's pattern, reveal no more of themselves than they did then, building instead on the tracts they have discovered, creating new selves daily, as their feet create fresh prints in the same sand. They choose their personalities whimsically, act out small lives while walking. A changed inflexion, a weighted word, an 'I remember' said with a grimace, a sigh or a smile evokes a type of face, of person and of past. He tells her he is a doctor, that he has studied in the Royal University and has fled from a burdensome practice in Dublin. He tells her he is a cattle exporter from a family of Dublin merchants, the eldest in the firm, he will feed England on Irish beef for the war's duration. She tells him she is an actress, left here by a repertory company at the end of a bad summer. She tells him she is a governess, sacked by her titled employers because of an affair of the heart. He prefers the second to the first, but he accepts both, just as he accepts the quick movements of her features from liveliness to pallor. There is something blessed he suspects, in the very poverty, the elusiveness of each encounter and of their knowledge of each other. And the only measure of their permanency, of their perhaps having met in some yesterday is the straw mat in the canvas hut which from the first day she has left on the floor of the bathing hut and which no one has yet disturbed. It is like an arrow pointing to their one reality, their lovemaking. And yet it is a mat, the repository of his bliss, his belonging with her to a realm of feeling, beyond which they can never belong. Through that they meet on a plane that is as far removed from the persons they chose as are they from the sand that clings to that mat that hinders their movements. They move and are covered in sand, remove little clothing; it is cold. And each time money changes hands, money, the coinage that makes the exit from the hut more bearable, that leaves them both locked in an embrace, among just sand, sea and canvas, until their next meeting. How will I not die when it ends, they both wonder, and yet when he peels the ritual three notes from his pocketbook and when she crumples them into the pocket of her fawn coat the wonder vanishes.

He is certain that he loves her. He is just as certain that outside the curve of this sea and the soft gloom of this bathing hut his love has no meaning. She is an event outside time and yet rooted in the most sordid of times, among the most precise objects.

'Is the war going to end?' she asks.

'No,' he says, and while beyond this sand the thought would disturb him immeasurably, here it fades like a whisper.

'I love you,' she says.

'And I love you,' he repeats. And yet both of them observe scrupulously the proprieties they have established for themselves. And neither feels regret since all regret, every sorrow, was implicit between them from the start.

6

'**M**Y MOTHER SAID that seeing both of them again was like seeing ghosts of what they had been—'

⚝

LOVE IS THE word Michael thinks of all the time, that unique syllable that takes in tongue, lips and teeth. He says it as he walks, like a hymn to the fall of his steps, he forms it silently with tongue, lips and teeth while taking newspapers from the hall stand, he hums it while reading them in the oak lounge. The syllable carries him off for hours, he sees the sun has leapt suddenly from the lintel of the window to the third pane and wonders what has happened in between. It hisses from a dentist's gas mask, silences itself in the aching stems of the palm trees, laps in the waves coloured with oil that drift in at the farther end of the beach. He hears it in the rise of Una's breathing, in the 'Ta ra, love' of the fruiterer to a housewife on the prom, on the headstones of the graves he finds where the town ends and the road limps into a stretch of moorland, In Loving Memory Of, on picture postcards, secondhand novels and the slogans of commercial companies. He watches her breathing and hums a popular ditty, 'I left my love and leaving loved her more', he sees people in their waking lives dominated by it, is amazed by the tyranny the syllable exercises and each utterance of it leads him to the one place where its utterance is unnecessary—the strand, the bathing hut.

⚘

'STANDING UNDER THE long glass skylight of Pearse Station (it would have been Westland Row then) like ghosts of their former selves—'

⚘

AND IT WAS through it that he could tolerate the pain of his wife's pregnancy. He had known for some time that she didn't love him and what was for him worse, that he might never love her. And so he repeated the syllable and garnered from somewhere the inescapable sense of loving that would never leave him and that now reached out to every facet of that holiday town from its slate valley roofs down to its elementary sewerage system that disgorged into the sea some-where beyond the beach, beyond the spa and beyond the graveyard headstones.

⚘

'WITH THE CHILD between them, the strange spotted light you get on the platform from that crazy corridor of glass, the train still steam-ing on the tracks, like ghosts of their former selves, come back to the country, to the multitudinous relations, the connections everywhere, the miniature intimate city where they knew every face and every face knew them, where those who have gone away are immediately judged on what seems to have happened to them. She walked forward, left him holding the Moses basket, kissed my mother and confided to her that she would not have another child—'

                                    ☆

THE WIND BELLOWS into the canvas hut and its stripes bloom suddenly, and sag. Una's day is approaching and each of his meetings there lead him towards what seems to be a delusion but what he almost hopes might not be. She is lying flat on the hard sand and he sees his wife's condition implicit in her. He imagines her slim, starved body blooming, he moves his hand over imaginary curves, begins to treat her with elaborate precautions. He insists that she never leap from the promenade to the sand and that she always walk slowly. He wills her sex, her features on to his unborn child; her blanched face, her ash-blonde hair, her peculiar childlike grace, each movement so contained and satisfying. He doesn't doubt for an instant that he will have a daughter.

                                    ☆

'BUT IF MY mother didn't notice, there were others that did. But as usual with people and with gossips in particular, they get the sense of something out of joint but the sense they make of that sense is even more out of joint. If you know what I mean. It was on him the blame was foisted—though maybe blame isn't the right word—the mystique maybe, the question mark—it was raised over him and the child in the Moses basket he was carrying. A little back from them, by the train, coming out of the steam. They raised a question mark, but they asked the wrong question. Whose child, you see, was what they asked. They saw their Una O'Shaughnessy, already quite a minor celebrity, that kind of fame that thrives on absence and aura, and they saw this young man behind her, the intense awkwardness about him that would later become his hallmark, and their guessing centred round him. It would all later bear fruit in the rumours of Rene as the illegitimate spawn of some great lady, actress, society queen. But they didn't see the real blight. People never do—'

༗

THE PALMS ARE absolutely still one day and the sea is crystal. Once inside the hut, she asks him for money, an extraordinary amount. What for? he asks. They are both standing and his head touches the wooden laths of the roof. I must see a doctor, she tells him. He tells her that he can only withdraw an amount like that from his bank in London. This pleases her. My doctor is in London, she tells him, smiling. Outside in the ice-cold sunlight she walks towards the sea. She staggers at the edge and then vomits in to the tide. It is nothing, she tells him, it will pass.

He is going to hear Roger Casement speak, he tells his wife. The name echoes strangely round the walls, and seems to carry to the palms outside. And why do you want to know, she asks him, about rubber and blacks? Mr Casement is speaking about the war, he tells her, against the war. She can only assent.

They meet in the empty station and travel up together, shocked by the sight of each other against a background of trains, dining cars and passing fields. They realise how used they are to sea, sand and deckchairs. As if it is not they who are travelling, their persons seem to leave them and each gesture and word is looked down on from above, by both of them, from that plane where their meetings began. They arrive in London and book a room in the least shabby of the hotels around St Pancras. His London is different to hers, he realises. She is a stranger like him, but a native stranger to her own capital. They walk together to his bank in Regent Street, where they withdraw the amount she needs. He wants to accompany her then but she is withdrawn and evasive. She arranges instead a time and place where she can meet him in the evening. He watches her fawn coat, barely visible in the crush of the upper deck of a tramcar. He walks from Regent Street through a succession of squares, streets and circuses towards the club in Bloomsbury where the Casement meeting is. The sunlight glances off the fringes of the lintels, bleaching all the roofs. He arrives there to find he is an hour early and so decides to dine. He orders all four courses to while away the hour but barely touches any of them. He has no appetite for food, the word love courses through his mind like a cold wind, he sees her fawn coat on the tramcar, he sees the jug and enamel bowl beside his wife's bed. He is finishing his coffee when he hears a commotion outside and sees through the glass-panelled doors a group of men arguing with a police inspector. They have Irish accents and one of them, whom he thinks he recognises, could be the Member of Parliament for West Mayo. The commotion increases and blows are exchanged and suddenly there is a phalanx of policemen and between them is being escorted a thin man in a tweed suit with the air of a country gentleman but with a black beard, an incredibly ravaged face and burning, melancholy eyes. The man walks quietly, puts up no resistance and passes, with his escort, out of Michael's sight. He finishes his coffee, watching the arguing groups, their anger subsiding gradually now that the cause of it has gone. Is that the Casement, he wonders, who toppled Leopold of Belgium? He feels he should join that group outside but he cannot summon up the energy. He sits and watches as they disappear one by one and as the last words trail off. Then he pays his bill and rises, walks through the glass door and sees in the hallway that the notice for the meeting has been written over in a scrawled hand: 'Cancelled'. He passes into the street.

He spent the afternoon in a moving-picture palace. He remembered nothing of the story but the fact that it switched rapidly from dining-room to bedroom to garden and back. He thought of how depth and movement could be caught on a square of white. He thought of the canvas hut and the hotel bedroom, all pretence of distance between them abolished, and of the death of time.

Some years later he would see an ingenious set constructed by an American on the Abbey stage for a play in which his wife would be performing. It would be the sole performance of hers he had attended since their marriage and the last he would ever attend. The set would be built on a circular rostrum, like a merry-go-round, with a representation of the interior of a peasant cottage on one side and the Lord Viceroy's drawing-room on the other. He would watch from the back row during rehearsals, his wife standing in a shawl with a bunch of flowers by the door of the peasant cottage. And then, in a sudden transformation which always amazed him, the set would slowly slide, the cabin disappearing to be gradually replaced with the Viceroy's room, the ball-and-claw tables, the sumptuous armchairs and the rattling cabinet of drinks. And there, behind the cabinet, a little in the shade, but coming more and more into the footlights as the set righted itself would be his wife, whom at that moment he loved, in a gown of lace and black satin, holding the stem of a wine glass. And he would be reminded of both his other rooms, how many years ago he can't remember, of the two people who inhabited them, while he would watch his wife walk down from the set to discuss some obscure point of stage craft with the American designer, while he would look at his child who stood before the proscenium arch, passing her hand back and forwards in front of the footlights, disturbing the dust that gathered there like diamonds. He would wonder what had happened to his other room, the canvas room, to the girl who inhabited it. He would realise that both rooms were in the end his creation. Within several days he would be shot and these memories would die with him, he having left to his daughter just his love of blonde hair, his sense of the other side of things and sense of coincidence, the cumulative history of her conception and birth.

But on the Thirty-First of January 1915 he walks back to the St Pancras hotel to find June lying on the small bed, a blanket pulled over her and her cardboard case on the ground beneath it. She is paler than he has ever seen her. She doesn't look up when he comes in, her eyes are staring at the ceiling. Did you see the doctor? he asks her. Yes, she answers and he knows something is wrong by the sound of her voice. He sits on the bed beside her and he finds that the blanket is wet around her thighs. He pulls the blanket back and finds that it and the sheets are sodden with blood. Don't worry, she tells him, there is always blood afterwards, less this time than the last. He goes to ring the maidservant but she stops him, tells him it will cause trouble, everything will be over by morning. What will be over? he asks her. Don't you know what? she replies. He says nothing, but passes his hand over her face, her breasts, her stomach under the wet blanket until he sees she is asleep. Then he sits by the window looking at the dark square, turning to look at her whenever she breathes heavily. When morning comes and the shapes of the square have emerged from the mist he turns once more and sees she is awake and looking at him, but with sleep still behind her eyes. It's over now, she says. You'd better go. And you? he asks. She shakes her head. I will stay here, she says. With friends. He goes to the bed and kisses her once and her mouth responds but her eyes close suddenly, as if their opening had been simply a dream.

On the train back he thinks of nothing but the passing fields. At the station there is a maid, who tells him his wife is in labour. And the child is born with him watching, holding the curved jug above the enamel basin which is swimming with blood and water, from which the midwife wrings towels, continually.

7

S O RENE WAS born on the First of February 1915, St Brigit's
day, across from the promenade which would have been by
then quite empty of umbrellas.

⚶

'BUT WHY CALL her Brigit when the whole point of their stay there
was to hide the fact? Una reached Dublin three months later and
even then she claimed the child was premature. Which was how the
myth grew up of Rene's extraordinary eyes and hair, her miraculous
maturity. The child they saw in that station, whom Una claimed was
at the most two weeks old was in fact a three-month-old bundle of
vitality. I would say she was quite a tender mite, a fragile copy of the
father, with blue eyes and hair that even at that age showed its blond-
ness. No wonder they were all amazed by this two-week-old marvel
with a straight, intelligent stare and hair that didn't stick to its crown
like some black secretion but stood up, half-blonde, and even dared
to curl. For her first few months she was a source of constant amazement among all those who saw her, a disjointed sense of awe and
misapprehension was foisted on her which was fed of course by her
mother, terrified that they would discover that this wonder of hers

had been conceived out of wedlock, maybe in an Amiens Street hotel after a Conradh na Gaeilge meeting. I discovered this later through a First Communion form and a senile nun who didn't notice any difference. I mean, beautiful as it is to be born on St Brigit's day, the advantages are more than outweighed by the stain of illegitimacy. Which is why they stayed in England in the first place, why they took three months to travel home. And why they arrived in Westland Row Station carrying her in a Moses basket like a two-week-old.'

꙳

STANDING IN THE corridor of glass with the escaping steam behind him, holding the head of the wickerwork basket and his wife still half-hidden in the steam, would he have shown the germ of the person he would later become and if he did would anyone have noticed? The knot of family, cousins, friends and half-friends, they stood beyond the steam waiting for it to clear. He watched their shapes emerge, moving to embrace him.

The steam died round his boots and he carried the basket behind her. They seemed like any couple. There would have been a passing sweetness in being home, greater than their differences. He quickly ensconced himself in his father's legal practice and helped to make it one of the leading firms in the city.

And she, Lili, if I have heard you correctly, began again where she had left off and rose to become the star of a new style of theatre, peasant in emphasis, nationalist in theme. She resumed her Irish classes and acquired an enviable *blas*. Her hair, which was of that arresting blonde shade that people would later remark on in her daughter, she dyed black. The eulogies to her talents in the papers of the time (with the exception of the *Irish Times*, which was Unionist in politics) are so frequent that they are hardly worth quoting. Suffice it to say that the qualities critics found to praise in her were sociological rather than aesthetic. She was praised for her 'modesty of bearing', her 'passion of utterance', but most of all for an elusive quality which was referred to variously as her 'Irishness', her 'Gaelic splendour', her 'purity of soul', a quality which, the *Freeman's Journal* claimed, was 'representative of what is best in Irish Woman-hood'. And thus, in one of those qualitative confusions which are perhaps inevitable in an emergent drama, not to mention an emergent nation, her public praised her as if she were the part itself.

8

S HE IS SEEN in frieze, as it were, on an impromptu stage in what looks like a drawing-room with elegant French windows. She is holding a spear and she has her head thrown back, her marvellous hair bound by what seems to be a leather cord. There are two youths on either side of her, dressed in pleated skirts which could be Grecian but for the elaborate Celtic signs emblazoned on them. And all three are staring towards what must be the cowled head of a photographer.

火

SHE IS IN a peasant shawl, with a flat behind her depicting the gable end of a thatched cottage. The drawing-room is larger and more sumptuous and the flats are bounded by a heavy brocade curtain, covering, I have no doubt, a set of even more splendid French windows. Her head is raised and her eyes are blazing with a kind of posed defiance. To her left is a figure with a grotesque false paunch and a large top hat bearing the legend 'John Bull'. This figure is glowering, over her shoulders, towards an equally caricaturish figure on her right who can be taken, from his goatee beard and his spiked Prussian helmet, to represent the Kaiser Wilhelm. And between them Una's fleshy arm is raised to point to a banner stiffly fluttering from the cottage's thatched gable. And the banner reads: ENGLAND'S DIFFICULTY?

⚸

AND IN THE last photo the drawing-room has given way to the interior of a theatre and the flats and the setting are more elaborate, though the scene they depict is even more decrepit. The scene is a room in a Dublin tenement in which a young man is sitting by a typewriter, his mouth open wide, obviously declaiming something to an unseen audience, his hand ruffling his unruly hair. I have no doubt that the play is O'Casey's first, *The Shadow of a Gunman*, and that the stage is the early Abbey; that the youth is Domnall Davoren and that the line he is declaiming is Shelley's 'Ah me alas, pain, pain, ever, for ever', with which O'Casey for some reason peppered the dialogue. Behind him, peeping over his shoulder at his typewritten sheet, holding a bowl of sugar, is Una. And I have no doubt that she is meant to represent the most ideal and fragile of all of O'Casey's heroines, Minnie Powell; and that her Minnie Powell was on the plump side and definitely too old. She was thirty-three by then, and looked it.

9

THEY ARRIVED ON the Second of June 1915. In the Easter of the next year there was a revolution. A Gaelic League colleague of hers named Eamon de Valera held Boland's Mills and was lucky enough to survive the subsequent rash of executions. His pallid face, his gangling, unlikely bearing, his tenderness for mathematics and his strict academic air had, Lili tells me, been the butt of many of her private, rather caustic jokes. But when the revolution (which surprised her, Lili tells me, as much as anyone, though she later pretended of course, that she was in on it all along) extended itself into first months and then years of gradually accelerating chaos, then open rebellion, she lent to it her sense of melodrama and backstage intrigue, discovered a sudden liking for the gaunt schoolmaster.

'And rumour had its heyday here, I mean that man who would stamp his unlikely profile on the history of this place as surely as South American dictators stick theirs on coins and postage stamps, the mathematical rigour of his speech, his actions, and her, who was fast becoming the *grande dame* of Irish Republicanism—not that there weren't others jostling for her place, but none of them had her advantage, she was an actress after all, a bad one maybe, but she knew how to upstage with all the cunning of her limited talent.'

How Michael became implicated is uncertain. Taking briefs at first, Lili tells me, in Republican cases and later assuming a full and active role in what would become known as the I.R.A. Una claimed it was at her behest, Lili tells me. I would like to imagine it was in remembrance of that promenade, remembering the affair of the bathing shelter, with the sense of holocaust, like the sea, all around them. His involvement gradually took its own momentum until by 1919 he had donned the cap and trenchcoat that characterised activists in the upper echelons of the guerrilla effort.

'Never got his name on a street. That must be to his credit. It'd sound odd, anyway. O'Shaughnessy Street—'

He took at one stage to writing verse, a practice that seemed obligatory for activists in those days. He never mastered Irish. His verse is somewhat painful to read, only memorable for the number of instances in which he refers to Kathleen, the daughter of Houlihan, as blonde-haired.

TWO

DUBLIN, 1921

10

I HAVE TO IMAGINE you, Rene, since he took no photographs. Una did, but only after he had died. You were three when you went to the convent on Sion Hill Road. You had a broad face for a child, eyes that could be seen as too small, but those who knew you didn't care. You were an ordinary child in every respect and what greater blessing can one ask for, than to have an ordinary childhood?

It's just your hair that is distinctive. Curls hanging all around your forehead. Your hair is thin but has a creaminess of texture that gives each strand its own way of falling. Flat near the crown but falling all around it to a fringe of spirals, like those clumps of flowers, the stems of which droop from the centre and the petals fall to make the rim of a bell. Blonde is a shade that catches the tints of the colours around it. Your hair is cream blonde and catches most lights and the outer strands make a halo of them. To have extraordinary hair is almost as good a thing as to have an ordinary childhood.

You sat with Lili on the small benches and the Cross and Passion nuns moved among the benches like beings from another world. Their heads were framed by those great serge and linen bonnets that nodded like boxes when they spoke. It is you at the time that Lili described, when your father would walk in in his Free State uniform and lift you on to one hip and then the other, trying to avoid paining you with his shoulder strap or his shoulder pistol while the gun-carriage rattled outside and the nuns whispered like a litany their offers of tea. You would have been near six then. And your clearest memory could have been mine. Of the beech tree in the gravelled yard across from the windows of the classroom. The trunk is huge and pushes straight out of the earth and the gravel is thick around it, revealing no earth or roots to prepare one for its intrusion. It backs in its magnificence against an old granite wall. The branches near-est the wall have been sawn off to stop them crushing through the granite. So all growth of branch and foliage is towards the school, towards the window at which you would have sat, staring. It is re-ally for you, the severed half-umbrella, the monstrous segment of tangled growth that shades half the yard. Across from it again is a small shrubbery, half-bald with grass, smoothed by generations of feet. A bell would have rung, a fragile shiver of brass notes filling the classroom around you, the nun's bonnet would have nodded towards the door and you and the class would have walked jerk-ily towards it and once outside you would have expended yourself in that circular burst of energy that erupts from nowhere and ends nowhere, scouring the gravel with your feet, the air filled with a patina of cries that seemed to hover above your head. Only when you had exhausted yourself would you lie by the tree. But the tree would renew spent energies, would gather a ring of small bodies around it, each newcomer jostling to rest her back against the bark. You would have won Rene, continually won, by reason of that quiet ignorance of the turmoil of others which would always have found its few square feet of bark. The bark moulded in scallops, rougher than skin is.

Your name would have brought you some attention among
the Eileens, Maureens, Marys and Brids. Two thin white vowels,
strangely unIrish and yet so easily pronounced, as if more Irish than
the Irish names. Your father's visits would have brought you more.
Most of the nuns would have baulked at the excesses of the Troubles
but would have supported the Free State side and have been overcome by the mystique of your father's name. He looks a little like a
statue, standing in the doorway. Two of them, though, would have
refused to be impressed. One from Clare, with Republican connections, whose tight mouth whenever she passed you in the corridor
would have said enough. And one old, quite beautiful creature, an
avid reader of Tolstoy, who would have regarded the presence of
gun-carriages in a school yard as an immoral intrusion. She is old
and tall, like a long translucent insect underneath her habit. The
thin bones on her hands and the shining white skin on them and
her cheeks, which is all you can see of her beneath the black, seem
to contain more reserves of energy than any of the younger novices.
Her hands are hardly warm, they hardly linger on your hair for more
than a moment; each of her movements is as brief as it can possibly
be, as if her body is reserving itself for a boundless, ultimate movement. And the reserve, the iron quiet that she imposed on her life has
had its recompense in the cheeks that face you at the top of the class,
as smooth and pallid as those of a young, inactive boy, in the grey
eyes under the black and white bonnet which reflect the impersonal
rewards of a lifetime's confinement. Her presence is hypnotic, as are
her maxims. 'Keep your hands,' she tells you, 'to yourself. Keep your
hands from yourself.' You cannot understand the contradictions of
this dictum, but through your efforts to understand them it assumes

a sense of truth that is, for you, greater than words. It hints at the mystery behind movement and gesture. You say the maxim to yourself in situations that have nothing to do with hands. You know the ideal is hands folded and demure on the lap of your unfolded legs, neither to nor from yourself, and you know too that this is not the final answer which, you suspect, has nothing to do with the dimpled, fleshy hands before you. Are there other hands, you wonder, unseen ones which these real hands must train to lie at rest, ready to suddenly bloom into a gesture of giving? The hands of the soul, you think, and stare at the nun who has repeated her maxim once more and is sitting, hands unseen, at the top of the classroom. Her name is Sister Paul and it expresses that maleness which must be the ultimate goal of her sisterhood.

Lili is your seat-mate. She is pert and alive, master of the social graces of that classroom. If anyone is the favourite it is she, catching the glances of nuns with the downward flickering of her eyelids. And even now I can see the small alert girl who would have arbitrated the loves and hatreds of that class, whose clothes would have been imitated, cut of hair, colour of ribbon, style of bow. She had a lisp and the lisp becomes in her an enviable possession. She is enthralled by you and your cream-blonde hair and yet can dominate you with her quickness and her tongue, for yours was more than anything an ordinary childhood.

You sit by the window and stare at the trunk of the beech. Sister Paul's voice wavers, like a thread held in air. Lili, to see the trunk, has to lean past you. You watch the shadow of its severed umbrella blacken less and less of the yard as the morning progresses. The first break passes and the second break, until the final bell rings and you

run into the yard once more and find your space against the bark and
if the armoured carrier is there, you are carried off in that and if it
isn't, you begin the long walk down the Trimelston Road home.

火

THE WIND SWEEPS down the long avenue, at one end of which there
is a half-built church in a new kind of granite and cement which
make the half-walls rise sheer and inhuman. How large it will be
and what a God it will hold. There is a group of boys playing near
nettles chanting 'Up Dev'. One of them is standing in the nettles, crying and leaping to retrieve his cap which either the wind or the other
boys have flung away. You stagger with Lili through the wind. It is a
spring wind and pulls the green of all the sycamores in the one way,
towards the sea. There is a line of coast houses behind you and the
sea, which seems hardly disturbed. You walk a few steps and turn
to the sea and then face the wind again and walk. Lili is laughing
and clutching her gymslip. The wind makes another sweep, you close
your eyes against it and a melody suddenly courses through you like
a long pendulum sweeping the tips of the sycamores in a heavenly
arc. It runs its course and finishes, and just when it seems past recall
it comes again, its long brass tones fortified by another one and you
listen and walk while the two melodies boom through you. There is
a rhythm of which each tree seems a distinct beat and the bass song,
too deep for any human voice. It recurs and recurs with each sweep
of the wind which pulls your slip against you, gripping your knees
and thighs as if it were wet. Then it leaves you finally and the wind
dies down and you are relieved. You turn once more to the coast

houses and the unruffled line of blue and then walk on with Lili, not saying a word. The boy has retrieved his cap and is standing near the nettles, smearing his legs with dock leaves, crying softly. Lili stops, looks at him as if she might console him, but then walks on. 'Cry-baby!' she whispers.

You walk past him, looking at his green-smeared knees. You have little that is defined or personal about you. You have not yet reached the age of reason. The melody flies and your soul waits for its return. You are like a mirror that catches other people's breath. One nun refers to you as that plump, blonde-haired girl, another talks of your slender, almost nervous quietness. You willingly become each, as if answering the demands every gaze makes on you. The most persistent attitude towards you is one of pity, touched by a warm, moral, faintly patriotic glow. You are the child whose father must rarely see her, immersed as he is in the affairs of the Free State, whose mother is busy, abstracted. Through you they see your heritage, the glow of newspring and newspaper reports, the profusion of rumours and heated discussions beside which you must seem something of an afterthought. You grow through the very stuff of those frustrated politics. You are Lili's most treasured possession, the prize that all her classroom graces have won her; though you are most at ease when unnoticed.

Are you already choosing between these images as to which of them you will eventually become? A choice that must be unconscious, but within which must lie the birth of real decision, as those glances we throw as a child are the breeding ground for the tone of gaze as an adult. Or are you, behind the screen of your ordinary childhood, holding each of them in balance, nurturing each to take part in the eventual you? For you did become all of them. You hold your hands folded, a modest distance from your body on the classroom desk. Your knuckles are still only dimples, but from those particular dimples a particular knuckle will eventually emerge. As you walk down the Trimelston Road the sea is always in front of you, a broad flat ribbon at first and then, as the road falls, a thinner strip of blue serge until eventually, when the coast houses rise to your eyes, it finds itself a thin, irregular grey thread.

火

ONE DAY THERE is a statue in the window with fresh yellow irises arranged around it in jam jars half-full of water. The statue seems frozen in an attitude of giving. The silver nun teaches you the austere beauty of its observance, tells you that this is the First of May, the beginning of summer, Mary's month. And all those girls, more than half the class, whose first name is Mary or some Gaelicisation of it, Maureen, Maire, Mairead, bow their heads and smile.

You look at the yellow irises, flapping in their jam jars on the sill of the window, behind which the beech tree can be seen studded with green now as if the month of May has hastily flecked it with a stiff green paintbrush. You can hardly isolate any one spot of green from the tentative mass but you still try, with your young girl's eyes, their imperfection of focus, their totality of concentration. The points which are in fact small buds and which in autumn will become broader leaves with the texture of beech nuts and bark resist all your attempts to isolate them, merge and separate and finally through the tiredness of your eyes become what seems to be a pulsating mist,

forming a halo, the limits of which you can't define around that unlikely trunk, much like your own hair, which you also must be able to
see reflected in the window-glass, and the image of your own blonde
halo becomes merged with the first green pulsating of the month of
May. You look from the confusion of yellow, blonde and green to
the black and white frame of Sister Paul's face, who is explaining in
her silver voice the intricacies of May devotions; how the name was
filtered through to light on half the female population of this small
nation, the class. You cannot know that your first name should have
been Brigit, Mary of the Gael. Sister Paul tells you that the class will
replace those flowers daily.

The narcissism that allows you to confuse the glowing strands
of hair round your face with the mass of half-formed leaves on the
beech tree, the yellow flags of the irises, is an innocent one and more
than that, an honest one, and perhaps even more than that, a happy
one; an unlooked-for gift that in later life will be the one thing friends
will agree is yours, that must have shown its first contours in childhood. Later that night your nurse bathes you. Her name is Madge.
She must have minded you since your mother's nights were divided
between performance, rehearsal and political meeting. She takes you
into your mother's room to dry you, wrapped in a towel, to the centre
of that soft carpet, surrounded by the mirrors of that open wardrobe, the dressing-table and the oval, quite mysterious mirror on the
wash-table with its enamel basin and swollen jug. The towel is draped
around you as Madge massages your hair. Then your neck and your
shoulders, and it gradually slips down as she rubs your stomach, your
calves and your small feet, until you can see yourself, naked and dry
in the three mirrors. Your stare has the concentration of a dream.

Your body is all dimples, the dimples of your breasts, your navel, your vagina, knuckles and knees. These will grow like the pinpoints of green round the umbrella of the beech, way beyond Mary's month, into the shapes of womanhood and you suspect this and your suspicion has the texture and emotional presence of the colours green, blonde and yellow that filled you earlier, but if it is a colour its hue is unearthly since you cannot picture it, merely feel it in the emotional centre where colours move you. Madge leaves the room to get your clothes. You are most attracted towards the mirror that is out of your reach, the oval one above the wash-basin. You drag over a chair and stand on it and try to see your flesh behind the reflections of the swollen jug and the basin. Your look is scientific in its innocence. You lean forward to see yourself better behind the white curves of the jug but you can't and so you stare into the water in the basin. You are reflected there, from above. Your face looms over your own cream expanse, shimmering in the water, your blonde curls sticking to your crown. You hear a gasp behind you and turn to see Madge aghast in the doorway. The chair totters and you fall, bringing basin, jug and water with you. You land in the wet pool and your elbow scrapes on the enamel curve and spurts blood. It runs down your belly and thighs, turning pink with the water. Madge runs forward with a stream of prayers and admonitions and grabs a towel and wrings it in the water and wipes your thighs and wrings it continually. She blesses herself with her other hand.

11

I T MUST BE soon after this that you reach the age of reason which, like the age of the earlier maxims, makes the undifferentiated flow of your experience manifest and outward, placing it neatly in language and time, allowing others to say to you that you are different now from what you were then. And though you wonder how such a change could creep on you unawares, yet when you hear Sister Paul explain the metaphysics of reason to the class (though she seems to be speaking only to you) you accept that you must be different if only because you are being told so. You accept that your days and memories up to this moment are one thing and after that moment will be another. You suspect a cruelty behind this knowledge though and wonder whether if you hadn't been given it would the same be true? She tells you how up to that moment you could not sin because you were not aware of sin but how after that moment the awareness of sin that she is handing you like a gift will make it possible for you to sin. And you accept a further slice of knowledge which defines this sense of difference in you, the fact that now every action will have to be balanced and passed between the twin primaries of sin and virtue, and that between them there will be an expanse of medial tones and that, no matter how fragile this difference in tone, there will always come a point where white swings imperceptibly into

black, beyond which you will be able to say, Now I have sinned. You
wonder whether this sense of sin is a gift to be developed, whether
you must learn to sin as you once learnt to walk. You sense that
these words she is imposing on the flow of your days are somewhat
arbitrary, like the words she underlines, for obscure reasons, on the
hymns she chalks on the blackboard. And yet there is comfort in the
language and Sister Paul has after all impressed on you that knowledge can never be useless. You toy with this new knowledge, imagining some use for it while Sister Paul continues with an image of the
soul as a droplet of pure water coming from God into the world,
tarnished only by the fact of its birth. And you imagine God then to
be a sea, remembering the water that splashed you from the falling
basin, for a droplet must come from some larger expanse and a sea
is the largest expanse you can imagine; you suspect that this sea is
not the sea you know, always the lowest point in the landscape, but
a sea that is placed somewhere above your experience, mirroring the
sea that you know, permeating you with its backwards waves. But,
Sister Paul continues, as our days multiply and as we progress from
the age of innocence to the age of reason (and here she pauses, imply-
ing a multitude of ages, the texture of which you cannot imagine) this
droplet becomes tarnished by the grains of hours and experience and
only our own efforts can wash it back to something like its original
purity. And you accept this image but fortify it with your own one,
of that ocean in reverse washing over every hour of your days. And
there is a slanting pencil of light coming through the window, falling on your hands, which are to yourself and from yourself, shaking
slightly because of the wind on the umbrella of buds outside, because
between your hands and the sunlight there is the tree. And Sister Paul

has continued to describe to you the sacraments that belong to the age of reason, those of Confession and Communion. She asks you to rehearse the reality. Each of you is to confess to her seat-mate the actions which, in the light of reason, can be seen to be sinful. Lili confesses to you a series of misdemeanours but the air of secrecy and confidence generated by your bowed heads is such that she ends with the confession that she loves you. And you confess to her another series and end with the confession that you love her. And thus you suspect a mystery in reason, sin and in the droplet of water far more bountiful than that which Sister Paul has explained; though watching her distribute the tiny pieces of wafer which are to substitute for Communion bread, you suspect she knows more than she has explained. And feeling Lili's hand curl round yours on the wooden desk you sense that reason, far from having tarnished your droplet of water, has washed it even purer and even more, has magnified it to a point beyond which it can no longer be considered a droplet, for such is the feeling welling inside you, you suspect it would fill a whole glass. All the other details of the age of reason seem ancillary to this: the Act of Contrition which Sister Paul writes on the blackboard, the pennies of bread which she distributes, which you place on Lili's tongue and she places on yours. And when the big day comes and you wear your white dress that comes nowhere near the brilliance of the yellow irises, when the events you have rehearsed take place, your real Confession seems to you a pale imitation of your first, rehearsed one. And perhaps you realise that the form of our public acts is only a shadow of that of our private ones, that their landscapes are just reflections and like that real sea below that imaginary sea, with its piers and palms and beaches, reflections in reverse.

火

IT'S SOON AFTER that that your father collects you, dressed in civ-
vies for once, in a tweed suit and a hat like any middle-class man, a
reticent figure in the doorway whom the nuns don't recognise, whose
daughter runs to him, whom he holds on his hip in the old way,
where she can sit comfortably for once. He carries her through the
school to the yard, her blonde hair almost matching the white flecks
in his tweed and there's a car there, a young soldier at the wheel.
You notice the soldier's ridiculously large cap, you stretch out and
tilt it to one side. He doesn't react so you stretch out your hand again
but your father stops you, lifts you over the door and places you in
the front seat. Then he opens the door and steps in himself, sits you
on his knee. The canvas roof of the car is rolled back. The young
man drives, but instead of turning right towards home he follows the
coast road, past the tall houses of Monkstown, through the sedate
sea-walks of Kingstown, up towards Killiney and the large mansions
with their shutters barred. Your father says little on the drive. He
asks you what you did at school and like most children, you tell him
nothing. There is a slight pressure from his large hand round your
waist which increases as you enter the wide sweep of the Vico Road,
which he remembers from the train he took with his six-month wife
and his three-month daughter, the Italianate sweep of which told him
more than all the brown fields and woodlands that he was home.
He holds his daughter closer as the blanket of sea disappears among
hedges. Her limbs have filled out and her eyes stare up at him with
a knowing that is independent of him but that must have come from
him. He comes to realise as the car speeds towards Bray how much

she has grown, between himself and the woman he rarely sees now, miraculously filling the absence between them, garnering her own life from the chaos between theirs. And the suspicion rears in his mind again with an elusive truth, with perhaps the last truth, the suspicion in Hyde Park, in the London railway hotels, in the figure of Casement being escorted from the club between a phalanx of policemen that the events which would take hold of him, whose pattern he thought he had divined at the time, were weaving quite a different pattern, that the great hatred and passion, the stuff of politics and the movements of men, were leading him merely to this child on his jaded knee, and that without this child on his knee those movements would have been nothing and would not, he almost suspects, have taken place.

This is Bray, he tells her, you have been here before, and she accepts this information and stares, as the driver turns left off Main Street at the promenade. There is a tiled walk and railings to one side and below the railings, a beach. There is a line of hotels to the right with a striped canvas canopy over each porch. He motions the car to a halt and tells the driver, whom he calls Jack, to wait. He takes his daughter's hand and walks along the prom and the clasp of their hands is tight and warm as if they both feel, in their different ways, at home. He leads her to an ice cream stand, outside which there is a board, arrayed with postcards for sale, each postcard bearing a picture of the sea front. She shakes her head when offered an ice cream, and so they walk on, her hand bouncing off the railings as if trying to grasp the beach. He misses the canvas huts lining the sea's edge but realises they are out of fashion now, their usefulness outlived, since the stray bathers are undressing in full view of the promenade. He considers the same question as he walks, remembering the sweetness of his bathing hut, of the woman to whom he has long stopped send-ing postal orders. He wonders which is the greater event, his encoun-ter with her or the war of that year, this walk along the promenade or the Treaty bother. They have reached a line of sad Edwardian façades which sweep from the town to make a right angle with the prom and on the patch of green in front there is an old man painting. Rene stands behind the man and stares at his dabbing brush. Michael stands behind Rene. He can tell even though the picture is half-fin-ished, even though he rarely looks at paintings, that this one won't be good. But the picture still moves him. It is of a shoreline and sea, but not the sea towards which the man is looking; his sea is a brilliant blue while the real one is dull metal, grey, and it is lit by a dazzling, garish light that could belong to Italy or Greece, but not to Bray. The naive sheen of those colours seems to come from a sea the old man carries with him. He has a shock of white hair, a high stiff collar and a grey-black suit baggy round the knees, that balance between fine cloth and shabbiness which could be termed Bohemian. His concen-tration on the canvas has a slight pose about it, as if he is conscious of the figure he cuts and of them watching. And sure enough, he turns to them suddenly without halting the dabbing brush and tells them in a gruff, Protestant voice that they are blocking the light. Look by all means, the painter says, but leave me my light.

The beach has finished now and the promenade has tapered into a small stony walk between the hulk of Bray Head and a rocky sea-line. They veer from the walk and go up through a field to the termi-nal point of the chair-lift. Will we go up? he asks her while a yellow chair bears down on them, swinging on its metal rope. She nods, as any child would. We went up before, he tells her, climbing up the metal stairs and into the chair, you, your mother and I. I don't remember, she tells him, settling in beside him. You were asleep, he answers, in a straw basket. The chair lurches into motion and bears them up, the wind whistling more as it rises. He points out Greystones, the Sugarloaf, Dublin and the road of her school. She stares at the painter below on the prom. I would like to stay here, she says. But you can't, he tells her, the car must go down. I could fly, she replies, if I wished hard enough. She stands in the swaying chair, her arms stretched out. Maybe you could, he tells her, looking up. And it is there, when the chair is at its highest point and the cables begin to sag again, that he stands and holds her, he is overcome, he lifts her to his chest and gasps over and over again the same few words. You are my child, he says, the chair swaying with him standing, and her. And you feel yourself lifted, you feel his sharp bristle at your cheek, the trunk of his chest against yours and his words that seem weeping and ageless course through you like that melody and like a child too you are embarrassed, you are even stiff, you feel his ribcage crushing you and you understand, when you find your cheek wet with what must be his tears, you understand how much of the age of reason you have reached. And the chair-lift lurches to a halt and he lifts you down and stands you on the bare Head, the grass scoured by so many sightseers, and he lifts you again on to his shoulders, your bare legs round his neck and begins to walk downwards. Always, he tells you, love your mother. And you promise you will, looking over his bobbing shoulders at the paddle-boats below.

12

T HE GRANITE WALL was still there, too big really, leaving only the lip of a path along which I could walk. I came to the new gates and passed into the yard, which was covered in tarmac. The tree was sprinkled with green, it being May again, and was leaning backwards towards me, having years ago lost its battle with the wall. There were prefab huts to my right where the shrubbery should have been. There was the old building still though, and the classroom, the window glinting towards the sycamore. I rubbed my cheek against the bark. Rene climbed it on her First Communion day, for obscure reasons. She couldn't have scaled the trunk so she must have walked along the wall and stepped on to the higher branches. There is still the problem, though, of her scaling the wall. A good six feet. Did she ascend into the heaven of the branches? Upwards through the air, turning reason on its head? Her dress would have been white enough. My cheek, as hairless as hers must have been, I scraped it on the bark, moved away and knocked on the heavy wooden door. I explained who I was to the young novice who answered. She had pale skin with a red flush in each cheek, dark hair and pale blue eyes. She could well have grown into a tender, iron-willed innocent of seventy and her adopted name, when she came to take her vows, could well have been Paul. She brought me down a small corridor, talking technicalities. I told her I wanted to observe, nothing more. She opened a door on the left and led me to a classroom. It was indeed the classroom. Twenty young girls turned their faces towards me. There was a dappled green light coming through the window. I placed my back to it, stood there and observed. The novice didn't teach and the girls didn't sit in their desks. They moved around on impulse, took out boxes of equipment, quite bland with freedom and self-possession. We use an open day, the novice whispered. Behind me there was a statue, wedged between two iris-filled jam jars. I tried to observe, but couldn't resist the temptation. I took one, sniffed it, placed it blandly between my leaves. The beads of water clinging to the stem smudged the ink of my notes. Take more, the novice whispered, we renew them daily. But one was enough.

⚐

YOUR ARMS AROUND the bark and your white front stained with that green pollen. Sister Paul paces the gravel six feet below asking how you got up there. You say nothing, immune to reason. She tells you the priest is here, the other girls are assembled. The tree holds you more than you hold it, your feet wedged in its umbrella. Come down Rene, she says softly. You have your head turned, looking towards the blanket of water. She walks away across the gravel and comes back with your father. He is in his tweed suit, immaculate. He holds his hands up to you, open, waiting to receive. You don't so much fly as float down. Your white dress balloons upwards. His hands grip your waist and ease you to the gravel. Sister Paul strides towards the chapel, billowing black. Inside the girls are white, lining the oak benches. All the lace is stiff and the bonnets are tied. Their breath rises like steam, to the high coloured windows. You walk down the aisle with him, your dress smudged with the green hand. The chapel is so intimate the statues could be real. You walk past the group of adults towards the priest on the altar, knowing your mother is somewhere on your left-hand side.

火

HE CAME DOWN the Head carrying her on his shoulders, down by the rocks and grass to the promenade, where he found his driver waiting. 'Home, Jack,' he said and they drove past the bandstand and the hotels and away again. Within the month he would be dead, shot on his way down Trimelston Road to what the newspapers said was early morning Mass but to what I suspect was the Booterstown seafront. The last she would see of him would be at her Communion, and for her Communion breakfast they returned to Bray, to the Seaview Hotel. Lili accompanied them. There, on a veranda which opened out on to a garden which led to a private beach, they ate grapefruit and cocktail sausages. Lili remembers the atmosphere as 'formal'. Rene's father was disconcerting in his impulse to please.

火

THE SCRAPES OF butter on your plate, yellow and whorled, beaded with drops of water. You shake the drops into your palm before spreading.

火

IT WOULD HAVE been a quiet breakfast. Her parents sit and watch the sea and let its sound be the only speech between them. And this is enough, strangely, for all four. For the girls the sense of occasion and the cocktail sausages are pleasure enough. And her parents had long allowed other facts to compensate for what was missing. Separately, each would have chatted blithely to their daughter. Together, they must make do with silence, and the waves.

⚝

THE WAITERS WOULD have recognised them. The scattering of other couples with their children in Communion white would have recognised them too. For Una was at her peak in her thirtieth year on the Bray veranda, enjoying, with the fame that had long been familiar to her, a sense of lithe aristocracy. An aristocracy all the more sweet in that it was an ad hoc one, its precedents changed daily, it combined the tone of ascendancy with the moral comfort of nationalist conviction and it was unburdened, as yet, by any sense of lineage. Una's mastery was total, though her glory would be shortlived. She was an actress after all. Her husband was known to have refused several portfolios. She was Republican too, wedded to the Free State. But this, Lili tells me, only gave her the added lustre of uncertainty, allowed her to carry through the days of stolidity the romance of the days of ferment.

⚝

SO I SHALL see Una in a dress as white as her daughter's, with a wide-brimmed hat and veil. He is in a less flamboyant, though immaculate, tweed suit. They eat quietly, listening to their daughter's chatter. And when the young waiter replenishes the grapefruit and the sausages he treats them with that mixture of deference and familiarity that their public selves project. He is Republican, this waiter, he is anti-clerical and left-wing. And yet, when back inside the kitchen he hears the old cook spit the term 'Redmondite!' into the saucepan, he turns and raises his voice in defence of the family outside with a violence that surprises him.

火

LILI WOULD HAVE her use this term. And others like it. She'd have her glorying in her activism, reacting to the split like the Republican she claimed to be. 'The one marital demand he ever made on her— that she keep her mouth shut in public.' Keeping her mouth shut, her presence felt. Swathing in her dark cape and pillbox hat through Republican functions, Gaelic League meetings, de Valera attending her opening nights. Having it both ways. Married to the one char- acter on the Free State side with 'an ounce of popular charisma', keeping up her old politics, her taste for intrigue. 'And it is a taste, believe me, a habit; which is probably why, of all the Treaty figures, he was the least vilified.' Dropping dark hints everywhere about sub- tle, back-room influences on him, influences 'not wholly political'. Fulfilling both her taste for intrigue and her taste for the public stage, having and eating her cake in this conflict turned increasingly vicious, from assassination to assassination, building a mystique round him that was in the end above politics. So when the end did come, she was in a unique position, having gathered about her that last element necessary for nationalist sainthood—the odour of graveyards. And by means of a graveyard gesture, uniting her public and private self. 'Mick,' she would proclaim to the handful of mourners, 'was a Republican . . .'

࿎

SITTING WITH LILI, staring at the cascades of butter, piling them on to the steaming sausages and as was only natural for a girl of your age, quite uninterested in the grapefruit. The young waiter takes them away, ventures to touch your hair, glancing at your father. The old cook spits into the saucepan. Guests catch your eye and give you sixpences, much to your mother's disgust. The taste of the wafer is still in your mouth, the perspiration of the priest's finger which placed it on your tongue, and you eat maybe to forget it. Una looks at the green hand on your white where the tree stroked you.

'Why did you smudge your dress, dear?'

13

MICHAEL WAS SHOT while walking down Trimelston Road, near to a church. He was not in uniform. He died quickly for, as was explained at the inquest, enough bullets were used to stop a running bull. Rene learnt of it when driver Jack came to the door without him. The wind sang the melody, beaten out by the separate trees. It is too much to believe that he died thinking of the promenade and the bathing huts.

※

'FOR A YEAR she was the *grande dame* of them all. But who could live up to the memories she invented for him? As time went on she gradually relapsed into what she always should have been—a mediocre actress. But she had a year of grace as the nation's widow. And that was a part. Her black cape and her veil were obligatory at High Masses, state receptions, public funerals. And opening nights. Never forget them. Rene was often with her, dressed in black too. But she couldn't just play the part, she needed a sub-plot. She made ambiguous references in public about how he died. She started hinting at plots and counter plots and counter-counter plots. She gave herself the air of knowing "certain facts" not available to "the public at large". Facts, moreover, which implicated those "in power" at the "highest level". She couldn't let it rest. I mean, everyone must have known there was a war on. She made it the done thing to give the air of being in on her secret. The ladies who copied her dress began to copy her way of standing at public functions with this removed, aggrieved, defiant air. The implication was of course that those functions had no constitutional validity, that *she* graced them with her presence, as her late husband had graced them with his life. She began to refer to him by the letter M. As M. used to say. Handy, I suppose, a bare letter is as anonymous and distant and mysterious as you want to make it, I suppose. I'd hear it in drawing-rooms, not knowing who it meant. You sense these things and you learn more of them. But it couldn't last, could it?'

泰

THE TWO OF them in black, on the sofa that whorls like a shell behind them, that seems to have been green velvet. The edges of the print are faded again by time, like a flame. Their figures stand out in what is an oval of light, or focus, the mother's hands on her daughter's shoulders, the sofa whorling out of the frame. There seems to be dust around.

泰

'AFTER A YEAR they stopped listening, didn't they? The more strident her claims became for him, I mean, the more embarrassing a figure she became. And by that time even Dev was looking for a way

into the second Dail. And so she wheeled round towards the worst
fate of all—that of not being taken seriously. And it often happens to
public widows. It began in what she would have called the "highest
circles", where the bow of deference changed to the nod of indifference, and it spread gradually, like a mild disease. In the end it hit even
her audience and real parts—by which I mean theatrical ones—began
to pass her by. But she never lost the indefinable air of being a figure
of consequence, and as theatrical circles are more loyal than most,
she kept her camp followers. Still, she found herself slowly excluded
from that magic circle of rumour, clandestine meetings and Chiefs
of Staff until in the end Dev himself didn't turn up at the opening
night of *The Moon on the Yellow River*. Needless to say, she reacted
in turn, she learnt phrases like "betrayal of the cause", "the true
constitution" and when eventually Dev came to sign that book of al-
legiance to the King with his left hand over his eyes, she condemned
him more vociferously than anyone. But by then people had almost
forgotten who she was. Una who?'

火

THE MONTHS AFTER the Communion breakfast are hardly memorable. The irises in the jam jars wither and before Sister Paul throws
them out you filch one for your copybook, where it smudges the ink.
The tree changes from green to golden and then finally empties itself
and you wonder whether this is what is meant by the age of reason
after all—a sense of absence. Then driver Jack comes and stands in
the doorway with tears in his eyes and his cap in his hand and you
see on the instant that this is one event that will distinguish this time

for you. You wonder what he is going to say. Something that will have the import of your father's words over the heather in the yellow chair. You look to Sister Paul for permission to rise from your seat but she anticipates the news from Jack's cap and his tears. She ushers you instead from the room, past Jack into a parlour you have never seen before, where there are oak chairs with slender ankles, green walls and a brown, glinting piano. You wait for Jack there, and his eyes and cap.

Soon after that you were taken from the school. Your education became sporadic. You would run on the Abbey stage now and then, in minor children's parts. Your mother, at the time of Jack's news, was appearing in a St John Devlin comedy, which broke all box-office records for a week. And it was in the Green Room of that theatre, the Abbey, that the photograph was taken of you. It was the first photograph. I can see you at last, your mother's arms framing your hair, which doesn't look blonde, since the print is bad. Your dress could be satin. It seems to be wet, clinging to your knees. You are staring at what must have been the cowled head and shoulders of the photographer and except for your stare, which is remarkably direct, you seem an ordinary child.

THREE

BRAY, 1922

14

A ND IT IS the spirit of that photographer that impels this book. James Vance, his passion for documentation, for capturing in a frame the shades of experience. Fascinated and maybe appalled by the wealth of his senses, did he take a puritan pleasure in sliding the print out of the acid bath, in seeing all those brash colours reduced to variations of grey? Or was the delight in the image ghosted on to the clean plate? As a boy, he hears Muybridge lecture in the Ancient Concert Rooms about his plates of galloping horses and wrestling men. He holds his father's sleeve, who queries loudly the airborne legs. But James just sees horses, as real as any that galloped on the Meath estate. And devotion to the magic of such images must have seemed a worthwhile thing to the man he gradually becomes. More than a pastime and yet less than a profession, since he had money, Lili tells me and his life, without the focus of necessity, needs its point. Does he grow with a conscience, Lili, a Protestant one, large and shambling, drawing him like a magnet towards all that he is not? And James Vance was unlike most of what he saw around him. So this conscience blooms, becomes like his person which is large and shambling, often ashamed of itself, ready to retreat at the slightest rebuff. His height comes to find expression in a stoop, his conscience in a constant apologetic demeanour which Lili claims was a kind of pride. History has decreed that he is more than mere Irish after all, and while his person seems bent on destroying this distinction, his speech retains it. His accent stays with him like a bad lung. He would open a door, Lili tells me, enter a room with a movement that always seemed on the point of checking itself. It gave her what she calls her 'turgid' feeling. But it can't stop me loving him, loving his obsession with days, months and years, with time and all its alterations in the faces he loves, on the building he loves, on the country he loves, as high collars must have made way for double-breasted suits, Ringsend brick for Wall Street concrete, as the waistcoats and pampooties of Aran islanders made way for shiny overcoats and steel-tipped boots. I think of the perplexity of the eternal child, of the vanity of all his efforts, as he tries to suppress the windmills of time, change and chaos into an ordered progression of prints, a march of moments pencilled in days, months and years, the four corners of each stuck down with Cow Gum, six prints to a page in that bulky album, hard-covered and black, like a Bible. I love the hopeless faith of this documentation, I pity the lack of faith that makes it necessary. I see both of us trying to snatch from the chaos of this world the order of the next, which is why even now, so long from the end, I am tempted to call him 'father'.

火

HIS FATHER'S OBSESSION was for paint daubed on canvas. He could be seen around this time sitting on Bray prom, near the end of his years, trading on the fact, conscious of the enigmatic figure he cuts, furiously unmoved by anyone who stared, his black suit and boots and his white hair ('Bohemian') and the sea that he painted repeatedly, if it was not the promenade walk or the hotels on the road proper. Lili preferred him infinitely and takes endless pains to disprove consanguineous similarities. It is the difference, she claims, between photography and paint—

※

BUT TO GET back to the photographer, what I can see is his fascination with matters technical and his huge delight in that contrivance, and in every development of it. And even given what she sees as excess of humility, I imagine him taking a hidden pride, a sly pleasure in the mechanics of that black box. He knew its powers, how it worked. He would walk down the slums on the north side and plant the legs of his tripod among the turds and rotting vegetables and give pennies to thin boys to stand in attitudes of deprivation. I suspect he gave pennies because the attitudes of deprivation look so forced: he was a bad photographer after all, the only valuable thing about his 'social' prints being the buildings behind the faces. I can almost see the copper gleaming in the thin boy's eyes. So picture him, the Protestant who had exchanged his horse for a conscience, on the Gloucester Diamond surrounded by vegetable thieves and dissolute husbands and all kinds of brassers, attempting to keep his thin kids quiet for the length of an exposure. They would have heard of the way the image magically wafts on to the coated paper. They would have gathered, from those tenements without parallel anywhere in Europe, into a respectful half-circle, a good six feet between each of them and the youth with his cowl, the magic of technology fascinating them all the more because they were so unfamiliar with it. And among those on the other hand who would have disdained that magic—as they would have, I imagine, in the Abbey's Green Room—he would have been blessed with a magic of a different kind. For as he began his theatrical prints years later, he would have then been able to claim that sure sense of solid craft, that 'know-how', that abstract concern with detail which is the tradesman's defence against the leisured, the educated, the effete.

大

WHICH IS NOT to say that he himself wasn't leisured, educated or effete. On the contrary, by virtue of his background he could well have been all three. We have already seen his way of opening doors. If we open the door slightly wider we can see him in that house in Sydenham Villas, facing Bray Head, its left side towards the sea front where in his last years his father used to paint. The last in a series of houses they owned, all of them round Bray and its environs, the first of which bordered on Lord Meath's estate and vied with it as a house of 'quality', I can see its precise, peeling, shabby grandeur; both its inhabitants with the accents of wealth, with the bric-à-brac of wealth thrown in odd corners round those rambling corridors, with everything to do with wealth except the momentum which keeps wealth going. Their ambition must have wandered, generations ago, from the sturdy concerns of their Huguenot forebears. They once owned property in Bray, a small ceramics factory, a shop in London and another in Dublin. Someone had scattered delftware round Europe from there, renowned once for its blue and green handpainted lozenges, for its whorls and for the brittle 'ting' each rim would give when plucked with the thumbnail. But as the parsimony of fathers is changed to the patrimony of sons and the painter had inherited along with an income an impatience with the details of commerce which he handed to the photographer as an inadequacy, the shops were leased to thrifty chemists and the factory, which had shut one year now long beyond memory, stayed shut, stacked with layer upon layer of forgotten, unsold delft.

15

THE VANCE FORTUNE proves more brittle than that delft. It lasts with the glaze of its lozenge and the scallop of its edge intact to find its home in antique collections. But their estate decays with the symmetry of poetry leading to the photographer, a thin trickle of dividends and the house in Sydenham Villas. Lili claims James was half-hypocrite, with his assumption of the causes and tenets of the revival, that he had 'airs below his station' which she seems to think are even worse than airs above. But one can glimpse something different—the thin sense of despair, the slow irony of history that reduces the difference between his house and that of his Papist neighbours to that of a coat of paint. He carries that difference like his conscience, like a bad lung. I see him on the slopes of Dublin Bay, somewhere around Killiney, in autumn, when the eucalyptus bark is peeling, reeking with the smell of tomcats. The sea is viscous, metal-hued. That difference has preyed on him, it becomes an effort to walk upright. He has read Hegel, Marx, Saint-Simon and has glimpsed the sublime unity through his favourite, Rousseau. The exhaustion of his background seems to lift. He sees the tide of history, and people simply washed.

He must love that sea, he feels, he must welcome all its movements, and among them the ebb and erosion of his class. For who is more uniquely placed, he asks himself and almost shouts the question at the hillside, to give themselves freely, wholeheartedly to Nationalist Ireland? It is their very base of privilege and the decay of that base, the one shearing them of all self-interest, the other opening their eyes, that gives them uniqueness. Who? he shouts this time and the echo could shift rocks. It returns, without an answer. And so he turns and decides to accept. Typically, Lili might say. To accept the decay of his fortunes and the iniquity of them, to retain the paltry privilege he has left and to work towards the elimination of all privilege. He climbs the hill, peels off some eucalyptus bark and rubs his teeth with it. And as the flavour spreads round his mouth, draining all the moisture and as his tongue retreats from the flavour of resin, the question persists with him. He sees the neatness of his formulations, how he has followed them with his shambling rigour, only to be led back to precisely the state he was in when the formulations began. And is it simply the state, he wonders, that suits him best? Is all the agony of thought, he wonders, is it just a wheel that turns and changes nothing, however wide the circumference, always returning to where it began? The cones of eucalyptus are around his feet as he heads for the Vico Road, like odd excretions from those striped erotic trees. He kicks them aside with his high-laced boots, their heavy soles that could belong to an intelligent tradesman or a gentleman who aspires to be an artisan.

火

THE SEEDS OF those eucalypti were brought from Tasmania by what Victorian adventurer? A hill, weeping in a blue haze, the huge trees dipping from it, divesting themselves of bark in long fleshy stripes. The bark falling to earth at the trees' roots, steaming, each stripe like leather, malleable, even useful. And the temperament that could transplant such seeds, over continents and dips and crests of climate, to root them by this bay where the rain falls in sheets and squalls, never in vertical lines. Their odour of resin and tomcats, plucked from that torrid world to fill this grey one. I walk along the hill and chew the eucalyptus. It cleans the gums, cures colds and freshens the nasal passage. I could dive into that Italianate bay, the erotic stripes of the trees above me.

॰

IT WAS THE old man's temperament, impatient with geography, seasons, seas, impatient with everything. His rugged Bohemianism and bad taste. His tweed trousers and laced boots that were like his son's but that scarred any number of parquet floors. His voice, that never lost the haughty gruffness bequeathed him by generations of dealing in delft.

॰

'I LIKE ECCENTRICS, anyway, and Protestant eccentrics most of all. I went with her now and then, when she visited the house. "How's my fashion-cover girl?" he'd greet her in that room covered in tobacco smoke and the stench of his illness. She always bore it better than I. He had a photo of her knees in silk stockings, taken from an ad in the *Freeman's Journal*. He'd pull it out and ask to compare it with reality. She'd lift her dress and show him. He claimed he'd never seen knees so perfect, given all his years with artists' models. And knees, he claimed were the pivot of the female form. There were rumours once—this was years before Rene—of a naked girl with her back to that bay window downstairs that faced on to the street. Of him bringing the habits he'd learnt in Paris home to Bray. Rumour flew the way it flies and grew in colour as it flew and it reached the parish priest as a story of a girl from the cottages on the west side disrobing each afternoon for filthy lucre. And so the priest knocked on every door in that labyrinth of artisan dwellings, interviewed each girl only to hear each girl deny it, protesting her modesty. But what else would they do, the priest thinks, these that keep coal in their baths, but deny it? So he upped and went to Sydenham Villas. And picture it, if you can, a hot day in May maybe, he in a black overcoat, his stocky black hand knocking at the door of Number One, the old man answering, the priest humming and hawing, muttering eventually vague threats about Catholic girlhood. And so at last it dawned on old Vance and the story goes that he grabbed the priest like an errant schoolboy, dragged him into the inside room and showed him, on a satin pouf, in a room misty with tobacco smoke, a naked, dark-haired and utterly bored young woman. "There's your Adam's Rib," he shouted and propelled him back to the door. "She's not under your jurisdiction," he fulminated, loud, so the whole street could hear. "She's Jewish." '

⚹

THEY COME DOWN from Dublin for three months of every summer, from the days when the railway was first built, taking villas by the bowling green, the young Jewish daughters walking on the prom, plump and olive-skinned. That's before the droves of Scots and their cheap weekends. But then the story of houses and towns is decay. From the heyday of the Jewish girls and the first Great Southern line. Would the priest have transgressed years before, would he have dared call on Vance without an invitation, without coach and four to take him up the long drive with its views to the left of the Meath estate?

火

'STILL, THE OLD man knew who he was. He didn't have to learn Irish, stagger into rooms with a look of pain in his face, photograph every Mick and Pat with snot on his nose and mud on his boots. You could talk to him, you could love him and not despite his being an ascendancy boor but because of it. And that's the tragedy, isn't it? James, with all his reservations, got the worst of both worlds. Brooding, you see, is always unlucky. The old man never brooded. James did—'

火

IT BEGINS TO rain. The water falls in separate threads at first and then comes faster, closer, with no wind to impede its falling. A tropical downpour. James leans against a eucalyptus, which is useless since the leaves of that genus are tiny and form a laughable contrast to the smooth sweep of its bark. He is soon wet through, with the rain streaming from the trunks and the drops hopping from the ground and turning to spray and the spray turning to mist. The air becomes fetid, the odour more resinous, as if the moisture is clinging to it and it to the moisture. He stares across the bay and sees the sheen of the water, for once without trace of current or wind, transformed by rain into an even sheet of hammered tin. The tart taste of bark is in his mouth and his gums are hot and alive. The water pouring down the skin of the trees is unable to dim the cream-coloured stripes where the bark has peeled, and he sees those stripes as unlikely murals, scoured by some careless finger. He feels there is a life sleeping in him, being awakened now by this odour of tropica. It is as if the rain has recreated the home of this bark. There is a hill, weeping in a blue haze, the huge trees dipping from it, losing their coats in long fleshy stripes. His tastes are mathematics and photography, his sympathies Republican, his background Protestant. He has entered a Catholic marriage and his wife has not long ago died, having left him a son christened Luke. He has a self that has always merely watched, merely waited and observed and that seems about to rear now like a tapeworm, pulled by this moisture through his opened lips. He stares at that hammered sea as if waiting for a face to emerge from that multitudinous pressure of drops, quietly, unheralded, each detail sculpted aeons ago, before rain and sea started, like those faces that form themselves on his metal plates.

Would he ever see that face? The meaning we demand from the span and the whole but in particular the surface frieze of the sensual world is never forthcoming; or if it is, not in any form that comforts. If it comes it comes too late, if it speaks, it is always in retrospect and the message he wants from the grey sheet of sea and the tepid air comes only when both have been dulled by memory and by time and when quite another message is demanded. And by then, besides, the rain has stopped, the sea is quite achingly blue, it washes another

shore maybe, another bay and the only fresh piece he retains is the
one he in fact never saw, that edged into his picture from nowhere;
that face, perhaps, or that imagined hill with its outlandish climate,
its quite imaginary eucalypti. And yet it still clung to him, a dogged
belief in surfaces. He would have even then liked to photograph that
scene, to capture that precise balance of elements, why the rain was
thus on the sea, why the trees made it mist and channelled the water
in sheets and perhaps it was precisely for that reason—that tomor-
row the sea might be blue and the air contain nothing but the odour
of dust and sunlight. And it could all be held then and pasted in his
black book on his green felt table and seen as evidence of, if nothing
else, the impossibility of answers. How it was, each print would say,
on *this* day, the sun hit Luke's face in such and such a manner, and
he was seven then, and longer than his years. This is Benburb Street,
another would say, in the great days of hand-painted signs. And so
the prints accumulate, each one a document of how, of a present
that becomes past as soon as it's developed and only through the future gradually reveals its secrets; the accumulation of them across the
years becoming a question mark, a dogged, nagging why? And perhaps he suspected as he gathered them with that fatalism common to
collectors that each one was the attempted formulation of an ultimate
question and that all answers are retrospective, and so it took months
and years of prints for him to even know what he was asking; that
he could never hope for arrival, at the most for a judicious departure.
And besides, he had a passive nature, he suppressed the general, paid
obsessive attention to detail; the kind of passive nature that, when the
rain stops falling round the eucalypti and the blue is out at last, walks
from the thin shelter they afforded and stops thinking of them too.

16

S O WHEN JAMES Vance entered the Abbey Green Room what
would your first sense of him have been? Vance, from the
Huguenot Vans, by now a widower, years after his eucalyptus, one
Catholic son at home in his Bray house; a grandfather inhabiting an
upstairs floor who was there and gone, there and gone. He walks
in with his tripod wrapped in his cape. There is his way of opening
doors, dressed in corduroy and braces. The stage hands are following him, holding an arc lamp. He asks them in a low voice to put it
down. You can hear him, however. People carry their worlds with
them. You can sense its shape, if not its precise features. You sense
the way people seem to know him and the way he seems ill at ease.
You have been sitting on the long couch under the portrait of the man
with the removed eyes for twenty minutes now. Una has been tying
and untying your bow, placing her hands magisterially round your
head, then striding round the room in her black dress. You know
how the long wait is eroding the public strength of her grief. You
don't mind her grief being so public. She knows this photographer
who enters, everyone in the room seems to know him, exchanging
those taut nods of recognition that imply acquaintance, not friend-
ship. The stage hands hold the arc lamp with a familiar, somewhat
contemptuous patience. You are mapping out the landscape, the long

stretches of hill and plain, the terrain in which your mother lives. It is a different world. In the two days since your father died she has entered your life suddenly and fully. You know it will be your world now. You have met people you have never seen before who greet her as old friends, who know your name, your age, your habits. You stare calmly at the creatures of this new world. They seem to you the inhabitants of reason, obeying laws of gesture and glance which must be reason's alone. You watch each new face and how each new face greets this photographer. He is restless and embarrassed and on the edge of the picture and because of that you sense you will remember him, more foreign to that room than you are. The man with the three legs and the black cloak. Your mother stares at him, leaning back on the couch.

'This was where you took Sarah Allgood?'

'No,' he says, obviously puzzled. 'That must have been someone else.'

'Now that was a photograph—'

Her tone is peremptory, with a slight edge of malice and implies a judgment on him. You sense this but cannot know that the tone is one that the bona fide Republican would always adopt with the fellow-traveller. There has been a history of tangential encounters at political meetings and Gaelic classes so they would now nod if they met on a street. They would rarely exchange words, however. You sense your mother judges him to be insignificant but don't know why. Perhaps because of his tripod, his cape, his box, every action of his seems to you to be important. You could not have known that this would be his forty-ninth theatrical photograph, that even as he is assembling the arc lamp the figure won't leave his head, seven sevens, his idle taste for mathematics telling him there's no significance in the figure, his aesthetic sense, always quickened by the imminent flash, insisting there is. So he plugs in the lamp, and mother and daughter in their dark dresses on the satin couch are lit by a white glare. It is the picture of the diminutive girl in the black dress, the cream-blonde hair against it, her eyes shut tight, her hands gripping the couch that prints itself somehow in the base of his mind, already a negative, so intense is the light. He rubs his eyes and looks at her clutching the satin, and something more than his aesthetic sense tells him that here is significance.

'It won't do here, Mrs—'

He tries to drop the sentence casually, for he has forgotten the woman's name. He can't believe himself, that name that has filled two days of headlines, the woman he knows by sight, that he surely must have talked to.

She has sensed, of course, and taken umbrage.

'Why not?'

She wants to be Sarah Allgood he thinks, turning away, mumbling something about refraction of light, pulling out the plug on the arc lamp. He is about to take refuge in more technical details when suddenly, blessedly, he remembers.

'Against a flat, Mrs O'Shaughnessy. It would hold the light better.'

She walks past him towards the door. He follows them, mother and daughter, through the foyer, through the dark aisle of the theatre towards the stage. The dust is circling and circling in what light there is. He is wondering why he moved them, what he is searching for. He places mother and daughter against one flat, then another and

gets the stage hands, whose patience is nearing exhaustion, to move
the arc lamp in a slow itinerary round the stage. By now he knows
that his forty-ninth theatrical photograph will have some significance.
The significance is already there in this girl's black dress against the
barest of possible lights. But will it seep into the print, he wonders,
and some impulse pulls him from flat to flat, dragging his tripod with
him. From this theatre, which he had always entered like a moderate
imbecile, so willing to be of service, he now brooks no complaints
from its stage hands or its leading lady. When she protests now he
answers with a curtness that shocks him. But it shocks her too, even
out of her stance of grief and she moves with tight lips and flushed
face to the next flat, the next floorboard to assume her pose once
more. But each flat is too dark for him and with the black dresses of
mother and daughter makes their hands and faces appear dismem-
bered, as if in a masque or a dumb-show. He stares at them through
the cone of light, alive with eddies of dust, the mother's strict image
of grief and the daughter's total lack of expression. The resemblance
between them that at first seemed natural, unremarkable, like mother
like child, comes to seem tenuous and then non-existent. Where did
that face come from, he wonders, and whose replica is it? A white
hand moves up from nowhere and brushes an isolated lower lip. He
cannot reconcile it, the auburn of the mother with the cream of the
daughter. And yet he knows the mother's hair could be dyed and
her round face must once have been slender. He thinks of the third
face, the dead one whose power is already mythical, and for him too,
since he never met the man. Do some faces belong to our heritage of
seeing, indescribable, being part of ourselves? He has seen her face
before, lit with harsh stage lighting. But when he says, to the mother's

annoyance, that the light there isn't what he needs either and when the group have ensconced themselves once more in the Green Room, the resemblance returns with the daylight, quite natural, ordinary after all. The girl is on the couch, the mother's hands on her shoulders, her white, plinth-like arms bordering her face. He can see the resemblance in their mutual opposites, those features that make the woman coarse make the child pretty, those cheekbones with the low forehead of the mother would have led in the daughter to ugliness, but with her tall forehead could some day turn to beauty. And the pose is natural and he cowls his head and squeezes, realising as he does so that he has lessened his demands. All he wants now is the ordinary, from her, her mother and the sofa beneath them.

She exhales to the smell of phosphorous and he raises his head from the cloth, bringing his thoughts with him, none of which she could have read. She will forget perhaps the precise balance of those moments unless she sees the print one day; and then the memories will have to do with her father, slipping like a horizon out of her vision, with her mother and the new world of which she is now a part. He will carry his memories like a penumbra, as will everyone who met her then. But then he will have the print. He takes the train home, winding just above the sea and below the slopes that hold his eucalypti.

17

H E DEVELOPED IT the next day, and a portrait of Dev, and so the blonde child's head that had moved against the black flat took its place in that pit and hoard of memories that might never be spent, together with the first smell of paint in his father's attic, the smell of waxed flowers on the altar of his first wife and the wind that whipped over the Clare election meeting, necessitating de Valera to keep one hand eternally on his soft hat. They rustled there, useless and unused, like leaves in the dry pit, waiting for the rain one day to slough them to the top. And perhaps a hint appeared in the negative of the depths which memory would lend, given time.

Three days later it appeared in the national dailies, and satisfied him. Surrounded by the black print that would be read by thousands, and the headlines 'Mother and Daughter Mourn'. And the dots the image was reduced to would have had the elusiveness of wraiths. Phot. James Vance, in smaller print.

火

HIS SON, LUKE, would by then have been five. Lili will tell me nothing about this man—she claims ignorance, but her silence smacks of jealousy—about his crumbling house and his thin trickle of dividends, his father ageing on the prom, his spouse four years dead. The word spouse conveys an image, a pale face, a hesitant bride in white, and love somehow absent. An Irish teacher, maybe, in the National Schools; a Catholic. James takes instruction for her sake in that faith that must have seemed awesome in its simplicity, its vulgarity and its threat that in the end each word might be seen to be fact. She promises a life to him, a union with that past, that faith from which his circumstances have removed him. It is a whim, more rootless even than his politics, but this whim bleeds into life and time and gives birth to Luke. He has bought her, using the most profound, the most suspect coinage. Her body awes him into an impotence that can only silence hers. There is a green rug, grass underneath, the sound of a river. There are the lupins and tulips, the dahlias perhaps, in the church where he marries. They have the same sweet, promising texture of those that litter the altar at her funeral. He marries at Easter and she dies at Easter. And Easter flowers I remember as stiff, coated with the stillness of beeswax, more solid than real, like the ritual purples and blacks of the Easter cloths. Its pomp, its frigid succession of colour, its hierarchic universe can only appal him, the green stamens and the broad spurts of leaves, like gushing water frozen round the dark heart of flower. Does she visit Luke from further back than memory, fold her black shawl around him each night? The boy sleeps below, the father above him. The wash of sea carries up the street to their windows. Each wave falls with a lack of finish.

18

B UT I WILL still have the Bray curate walking the Bray prom, from the sacristy behind the church on Main Street past the bowling green and the intimate brick of the railway station to the front. The wind whips his soutane there and dots the ocean with white and only the bravest of hotels have their awnings spread. Ultramontane, intellectual and too plump for his years, Father Beausang's nature is childlike and innocent rather than priestly. He has been visiting the obscure Protestant since the days of his marriage. His brief was conversion, then. If he asked what his brief is now, he couldn't answer. For the visits kept on, through marriage and bereavement and dropped all pretence towards instruction on the way. Until now they have lasted so long that the bishop finds them suspect. But yet, the curate insists, though this Protestant agnostic has not yet said yes, neither has he said no. And there is after all a Catholic child to be catered for, his needs all the more pressing since his Catholic mother died. But the truth is, he knows, as he walks along the tiles past the flapping canvas, that he has come to enjoy their conversations. Ethics, the moral law and the necessity of a credo have killed themselves as topics. Only the barest of philosophic questions are touched upon. Rather they weave themselves, one afternoon every two weeks, from initial and sincere pleasantries

through the fog of current events to the two subjects that alone interest them—mathematics and photography.

Years later I will walk with him past the flowered pots on
O'Connell Bridge towards the dried-up canal. He will talk about
maths with the same passion as he did then, with more passion even,
for by then his soutane will be flecked with snuff and dandruff, there
will be an unashamed smell of alcohol on his breath and his smile will
have grown wiser, more abstract and innocent, from the crooked,
sad crease that you photographed. Your arm is around his shoulder
in that snap, the open door of your house frames you, both of your
chests puffed out, endlessly amused because both of you, photographers, were photographing each other. You did it by means of an
extended puff-cord which explains the way your hand is stretched
out, a minor invention in the march of the camera soon to be made
redundant by the timed exposure, but one in which he would have
delighted in then, bringing it to you like a child, though your delight
would have been more muted, I suspect, since you were after all the
professional. That smile will light again when he talks to me of mathematics and tells me that God in His essence is a mathematical symbol
and that love is a figure like pi, the calculation of which never ends.

火

RAIN BEGINS TO fall on the promenade and Father Beausang quickens his step. You see him through your bay window, hurrying towards your door. The bay window is large, with a curved sill on
which it is pleasant to sit. It affords two separate views, one through
the left-hand curved panes of the Villas heading downwards towards

the sea and sloping towards the yellow chairs that crawl up the Head; and through the right-hand curved panes are the Villas again, rising towards Main Street. It is the window on which the Jewish model sat, naked on velvet cushions before the outraged eyes of the curate's superior. There is a table there surfaced with green felt, standing in the half-circle of the window. The light is always changing from the window so those who sit there come to know intimately the moods of street and landscape under the rain, the squalls and sheets forever falling on the bay beyond. In summer the window catches the sun for a full six hours. So summer is marked by a yellow glare and the yellow boxes of the chair-lift creaking towards the summit and by the bleaching of the green felt table. The quality of that room, though hardly remarkable, must have been constant, for Lili hated it, the curate when reminded of it grew nostalgic and I, when I visited it, could see at a glance what the one hated and the other loved to remember.

The drops gleam on Father Beausang's cheeks. His eyes are damp with pleasure and rain. He slips a book out from under his soutane. Luke comes down the stairs and stands on the last step while the priest ruffles his hair. You tell Luke to bring in tea and sandwiches. Father Beausang touches your elbow and holds up the book. You read the title and smile. *Arithmetic and Mensuration* by Eamon de Valera.

Once inside the unheated room, though, the book is forgotten. The curate has made a much rarer discovery—a French mathematician whom he came across, quite by chance, in the *Proceedings of the British Academy*. He tells you his theories and the sheaves of his person seem to fall away, his eyes illuminated, straining through logic towards what he hopes is beyond. You feel quite sad, listening,

anticipating his inevitable return. He relates an analysis of the process of mathematical research and discovery which, he claims, could
lead the secular sciences back to the point from which they departed
in the late Renaissance—to a recognition of simple illumination,
Divine Wisdom. He has as yet read only accounts of these theories,
has gulped them down whole in his excitement, but his sense of discovery is so real that it excites you, unwillingly, in turn. Poincaré, the
curate tells you, between hurried mouthfuls of cucumber sandwich,
sees mathematical research not as merely the inevitable unravelling of
applied logic but as a series of leaps into the unknown, for which the
light thrown by logic alone could never suffice. The logic, he claims,
by which the scientist seems to proceed could never suffice for his
journey. The very choice of an area of investigation eliminates an
infinite number of possible choices. And progress is made in a series of intuitive steps for which logic is the language but never the
instrument. And there comes a point, beyond that language, beyond
the resources of intuition even, at which the material amassed simply
resists analysis. The curate turns towards you, lit by the grey light
from the bay window. All resources seem to fail here, he tells you,
and the mind is just a filament, waiting for a current. He quotes a
remark by Einstein. The problem, stated and restated interminably,
harried over for months gives way suddenly, quite arbitrarily, like a
shattering mirror. The mind is admitted into the realm in which scientific discovery is made. And this moment is likened by Poincaré to
instantaneous illumination, a step beyond the realm of the rational,
through which understanding is bestowed on the mind like a gift . . .

⚚

YOU TURN AWAY from the dialogue to watch the rain falling in sheets now on the prom. You can see the snout of Bray Head nudging past your window, a thin strip of the promenade resistant to the water hopping off it and the broader band of sea which accepts the rain, mottled by the squalls. The dialogue has come round to that point you had hoped it would resist. This innocent, glowing cleric is drawn to it, independent of himself. A faint disturbance rises in you, the kind of upset that could be due to bad digestion, you want to fart and blame it on the cucumber sandwiches or the inordinate amount of tea you have drunk. His excitement has carried you with it. You sense it springs from your own perplexity. But your disturbance is more than gastronomic. You remember the stiff wax flowers of her funeral, the flowers the church was drenched in at your wedding, all Catholic flowers, a display of faith in the natural object placed at the heart of the human event, an insistence that those same objects are more than themselves, are symbols of what the human event pertains to, limiting it on both sides, the flowers that brushed soundlessly the first time and that stood stiff and waxed the second. And you wonder whether the curate's drift towards that point, the point at which these memories emerge and sidle towards you like forgotten enemies, to be confronted or evaded, is just an extension of his pastoral duty. Though your Tuesday conversations haven't touched on these things for years, his very presence is a subtle reminder of them. Your discomfiture gives way to mild annoyance. Some unspoken agreement has been broken. You suspect he has been breaking it all along. You resent being reminded, through the theories of an obscure, possibly dilettante French mathematician, of your agnosticism, your perplexity and your deceased wife.

The curate moves from the window and places his hand on your arm. You aren't used to hands on your arm, you are made as uncomfortable by them as by opening doors. But all you feel through his hand is the depth of his liking for you. This is another subject that has never been broached. Even that, the pressure says, will fail us some day. You look for words to answer him, somewhere between affection and faint resentment, but you can't find them. He saves you again, as if saving is always his duty. His words are like your flowers, hedging round that miniature human event. He mentions the book he has brought.

'I wonder, can Dev enlighten us?'

The door opens as he smiles. Luke comes through. You smile, almost in gratitude.

火

I WILL HAVE Luke open doors as quietly as James, but with the added ability to do so unnoticed. Like a good waiter, unembarrassed by silence, feeling no need to explain his presence. He has a transparent complexion at the age of eight, luminous eyes that stare all the time but rarely seek attention. The grandfather's bluster makes way for the father's reticence and for Luke's transparent quiet. The youth whom Lili met at eighteen implied just such a boy. You tried to imagine him, she tells me, as a boy: did he carry himself just that way when he was twelve, eight or ten? And the boy who possessed that odd intensity, that appalling certainty would, she says, have been an intimidating boy indeed. Her impatience with the boy's father is only matched by the rapturous approval with which she remembers the son.

So he comes in quietly to take away the tea things, knowing the discussion to be all but finished. Standing there, taking in with his eyes the rain-filled window and the two figures by it, Luke understands the embarrassment of the curate's gesture, he already knows his father's dislike of hands on arms and elbows. He sees his father in the window-light and listens to the opaque mystery of their conversation, the last soft wave of dialogue, those words of more than three syllables which characterise adult conversation for him, breaking to those pleasantries which for both of them signify an ending; though Luke doesn't grasp at the pleasantries but at the fading scent of the argument, at the curate's round diction and his choice of words. The words are new to him and carry an exotic allure. He is a thin, erect child who holds himself rigidly, a little like an older man. It's only in late adolescence that he acquired the look of youth that Lili characterises as 'slender'. Now he is thin and luminous, something aged about his silence, looking at his father and the curate, catching the drift of those ultramontane words. Their use is therapeutic for the curate, for whom the realities of parish life have formed a bitter contrast with his scholastic novitiate. They remind him of St John Lateran's College in Rome, of his first love, theology, and of his present ambition, to unite the logic of belief with the logic of science. They would have carried to Luke the germ of that *summa* which every utterance implied. Standing there, waiting for the pressure of the curate's warm hand on his father's elbow to cease, for them both to turn with that sense of finality which would be the signal for him to pick up the tray with its cups and remaining sandwiches and carry them outside. And of course they turn and Father Beausang and Vance look at the tallish boy with the brown hair flat on his head, sharp stickles of a quiff on the right-hand side of his parting which lend to the luminosity of his eyes an air of constant surprise. The curate thinks of his duty towards this child of a Catholic marriage, he probes the child's features gently as if to find some air of loss, of deprivation there. He can find none, however, and so he stretches out his hand and feels the stickles of the quiff with his palm.

'I have something for you,' he says. His eyes shine. 'If your father doesn't object.'

James has his back turned, his face to the window. You stare from him to the curate, whose palm has stopped kneading your hair. He hands you the book.

'Bless you.'

※

HE LEAVES, WALKS back out through the hall to the door and the rain on the promenade. The odd sense of maleness in that house, that hall, the rather bare order over everything, like a presbytery or bachelor residence, makes him feel he's leaving one home to go to another. The house was cleaned, but never softened, by a combination of three maidservants. There was a hatstand near the front doorway. And a mural, running down the stairway, covering the left-hand wall.

※

IT WAS A moving picture, Lili tells me, a sprouting forest of the old man's mental world. He works on it in bouts and then leaves, returns months later, having decided to change the theme. So stories run

through that wall in waves, conflict at each end and meet in the centre. Three muscular, bare-breasted women run downwards behind
the stairway, over the peeling plaster, towards the front door. He has
given the doll-like face of the local chemist to the one who stoops
for the apple while she runs. He has put Grecian hills behind them,
a Doric pillar, crumbling, in the left-hand foreground. But he must
have changed in the course of it, switched his obsession, got afflicted
with what Lili calls a 'bout of Irishness'. He changes the background
ruins into something like stone cottages. He adorns those hills with a
necklace of low stone walls.

꙳

AND THE CURATE moves past the bare breasts and the lesbian contours and the Hellenic pillars and the Connemara walls. James follows, leads him to the door. The hills at that end melt into blue, the
beginnings of a sea, Atlantic or Aegean. The curate opens the door
and walks through the rain to a view of real sea. James watches him
go. Luke clatters from the inner room with the tray of tea things.

꙳

LUKE MAKES HIS first appearance in a Moses basket surrounded by
a sward of green. There is a plaid rug there and a woman kneeling
on it. Of the woman one can see the bottom part of a gabardine coat,
hands placed deep in each pocket, one sleeve pulled back to reveal
a thin wrist. She must be looking at the child in the basket as James
must be too, with perhaps the same sense of approval. One can't tell

since one can't see her face, but James approved, obviously. The shot
is worse than most. He has ignored the simplest rules of composition,
as if his approval blinded him to them. There is no idea even of where
the basket lay, Powerscourt, Bothar-na-Breena, the Dargle Valley. It
is just seen from above, with the grass around it. James ignores the
woman for the child, who is lying on his back. His head seems to be
attempting to turn.

19

H E WALKS OUT himself, some hours after the curate. The rain has stopped by then. Does it only stop at night? The roads are quite deserted and the chairs on the Head are glowing like yellow moths, but motionless. He walks up the road and away from the sea front and the spaces between the houses become smaller and smaller. The road no longer merits the term Villas, becomes gradually a street. He has a longish tan gabardine coat pulled tightly round him, belted too, for the winter winds are in again after a summer of picnics and photographs, perhaps not too unlike the ones in which she appeared holding the baskets or prams, ones with large wheels that dominate the frame, as obsolete now as steam engines, graver than current ones with hoops, as on flower-baskets, covered in lace. The street has become a main one and the houses one wall of red-brick, one up, one down. He met her in the Gaelic rooms in Parnell Square, could never have met her here. The huddled square could well have housed some of those who worked on his great-grandfather's delft. There was a twig pattern with a necklace of lozenges for leaves that needed a miniature, feminine hand. A factory of women, year of Our Lord 1809, when the delft still rang across Europe, when the china dust still billowed in the workshop. Does he fall in love in memory of them, at adult Irish classes, Parnell Square? Stuttering through this rural tongue with his unfortunate *blas*, the eucalyptus chewer with the bad conscience, it is the gulf between them that attracts him as much as the person herself. There is chalk-dust in the air, without the billowing texture of the dust of china. But nevertheless the young teacher's fingers, which he wants, he needs to hold, are coated white. It is love, but always as an afterthought, the unique syllable lost among the consonants of Gaelic. Her plain dress is whitened in places as he looks at her over the row of benches through a halo of chalk. She has brown hair, blue eyes and an oval face. And when he comes to hold her chalk-whitened fingers which smudge his own in turn, his love gains the intensity of all his mental agonies. Her fingers are Irish, Catholic and youthful. He drifts towards marriage holding them, since he can do nothing else. And Eileen becomes Eileen Vance, with that unbridgeable gulf between fore and surname.

I will call it loving, though it was forgetful on his part and cruciform on hers. She doesn't so much age as contract under the pressure of that gulf. That terrible forgetfulness that never focussed on her face, that never caught the sunlight on its contours in the Dargle Valley or the Devil's Glen. He was kind, like all intelligent men, and therefore amazed when she began to weep one day on the Dublin-Bray train, where it brushes the sea just past Killiney. This child will be Catholic, she said, her curve outlined by the train window and the sea behind. Even if you won't. His amazement changed to perplexity when her weeping didn't stop. It lasted through her ninth and final month, until he could only wonder how so much weeping could rest in one person. It seemed to fill each room with an element not quite water and not quite air, but definitely liquid, through which he moved slowly and only saw her from a distance, until her weeping was augmented by her breaking waters and the pain of her delivery of their child.

Does he think of her, walking past the mock-Tudor town hall at the crossroads and out towards where the houses stop, giving way to the sweeping lawns of Lord Meath's estate? Eileen Vance. The name implies the lightness Lili sees in Luke. Her face that never slid into his frame but found itself reproduced in his only child. He walks down the road with a hesitant amble, a constant phrasing of a question too deep for an answer. He cannot but form it and so his fate is to seem wrong. He reaches out through the countryside, his body arching forwards with that curious perplexity, that gait that would probably irk anyone who passes him as much as it did Lili. No one passes him, however. Though there are footsteps behind him. And her memory is still in him, as alive as ever and just as abstract.

The footsteps behind him grow louder. He hears the clunk of metal on wood. He turns his head as he walks and sees a young man behind him, with a bicycle propped against an oak tree. The young man has a bucket and a roll of posters. He takes a brush from the bucket and pastes a sheet against the bark with one wet stroke. James stops. The youth cycles past without a word. James can make out a slogan and a bareheaded sharp profile, dampened by the paste. He walks back to it. There is a sharp aquiline nose, a rigorous mouth without a trace of humour, and a pair of wire-framed spectacles. The eyes on the poster reflect his own abstraction, and with it a quite terrifying certainty. They stare into the distance, embedded with the mathematics of vision. He watches as the damp spreads round the face. There is something foolish, horselike in the features which only adds to their allure. The corners of the mouth sweep downwards, in one clean line. James smiles. Years ago he photographed it, at a Clare election meeting. He sees those features and their certainty mould into the tree's roughness as the spreading paste weds the bark to the lettering. 'De Valera—*Clann na Poblachta*: Vote for the Republic!'

20

J AMES WALKS WITH Luke towards the photo with Miss Meredith, towards the tea it promises, along the railway tracks. The tracks loop around the Head, which looms over Bray and makes a gentler curve away from it.

But it is far behind them now, forgotten. James points out the marks of currents in the water, the glint of schist in the beach rocks, the banks of cirrus cloud above them. He explains the difference between flotsam and jetsam and the movement of tides. They come in view of Greystones harbour and the high houses behind it. Luke leaps from sleeper to sleeper, seems not to listen. They step down from the track and walk along the beach until the pebbles give way to clear sand and the sand rises towards the sea road.

Miss Meredith suspects that Mr Vance has intentions other than the sampling of her excellent high teas. She has the table spread when they arrive and they are the only weekend samplers. A widower who seems of her own persuasion, with one son cared for only by a housemaid. She has laid out her choicest dainties, cakes that are whorled with icing, cream puffs and apple-and-raspberry tarts. This Protestant gentleman, though, eats hardly anything, stares through the laurels at the haze above the sea. For today could be the height of summer and high teas are on the lawn, the lawn with such a riveting view of the sweep of the bay. He covers her white cloths with flower-samples after the ritual gentlemanly greeting, and talk is mostly of the weather. She has come to despair of a more active demonstration of interest. And yet there's the photo. On a day like today, with one arm around Luke and one hand touching the wrought-iron table on which lie the dainties. I feel I know the house and the way the garden looked at the sea. There is a low wall, white, that hardly reaches your calf if you are an adult but forms a barrier for a child. It makes a sharp angle round a little chink of lawn which is in turn hedged round by a large expanse of gravel, a sort of drive really, leading up to the house. There is a sign above the porch advertising teas. There is a thin row of laurel bushes parallel to the house, facing the road, and the chink of lawn is to the left of both, edging out on its own, for all the world like a small promontory jutting out to sea. For beyond the wall only the sea is visible. Your three heads outlined against the white wall and the white horses, the white metal table and the blue china, an idyllic scene as I imagine it, and perhaps you would have taken more notice of the notice she took of you had it happened oftener, but the weather so rarely allowed it. How Miss Meredith must have cursed that rain, sweeping interminably over Bray Head, knocking the boats against the Greystones harbour. But she must rest content with her picture in your album, her arm around your son, who is staring at the dainties. She is looking towards me, a rather fattish face, a closed smile in which the teeth could be biting the left-hand corner of her mouth since her lip is drawn down somewhat, slanting while smiling. Her hair is drawn back tightly like a Spanish widow's, parted in the middle and clutched behind into a bun. You could have been sitting on the low wall, your back to the sea and the white horses, over which hung the four o'clock sun.

﹖

MISS MEREDITH POURS you another cup and asks whatever happened to the family's china. She has an immaculate cabinet upstairs, she tells you, which must get more valuable by the year. You tell her there is a store of it somewhere, down by the old factory, most of it worthless, rejects. The time is gone, you tell her, for small enterprises and small nations. Versailles, you tell her, would have taught anyone the latter and the economy of contemporary Ireland would teach anyone the former. You hold such daring opinions, Mr Vance, it's a wonder you don't publish more. There are people better able than me to articulate them, you proclaim, and proceed to tell her about the Venus's fly-trap, which interests you more. But she evades the topic of the carnivorous plant and returns to your opinions, which in her normal day she would shun, but which with you she feels she must air. We are both anti-Treatyites, Mr Vance, but I have heard from opposite points of view. You are really a Republican? I would favour, you tell her, a syndicalist model along the lines of Proudhon—, Ah, Miss Meredith interrupts, but he was a Frenchman and respectable, quite a different specimen from your de Valera, who is Irish and disreputable. American, you counter. Or is it Spanish—

And your imagination wanders, as it always does when confronted with the intricacies of politics, beliefs that refuse to form themselves into any semblance of order. There is a boy leading a dray-horse down the street and the boy is barefoot and each step of the dray-horse's forelegs seems about to crush the heels of the boy, but somehow their feet move in counterpoint, a counterpoint whose rhythm you cannot pinpoint. The horse's paw-like hoof is raised

whenever the boy's heel arches backwards and each time the steel
hoof comes inexorably down, somehow the boy's foot just withdraws itself. Is it a logic like that, you wonder, that impels politics,
one that's understood just by boys walking abstractedly, by shop-
keepers, tenants and small farmers? You see de Valera's face flapping from every lamp post now, since the election is drawing even
nearer, and all around you, Luke and Miss Meredith on the chink
of lawn is the sound of paper flapping, his face flapping against the
tarred wood because a wind is rising from the sea now, a wind that
makes you aware of his face, of the time and of how cold you are. So
you rise and present Miss Meredith with a coin, which she refuses,
which you proffer again and which she refuses again until your annoyance at last becomes real, at which point she accepts. You know
that she would rather not accept, as you know that for you not to
give it would imply intimacy you don't want to allow. And so you
leave this woman whom you photographed as you never did Luke's
mother and you trudge across the Head again with Luke. Father and
son go back down the beach, beyond the sand, to where the pebbles
make walking difficult. There is a horizontal scar where the beach
ends and the land begins, above which runs the railway. As they
walk this scar becomes a cliff. The pebbles he walks over accentu-
ate his stoop. He talks about the rocks in the cliff face, the angular
movement of them caused by a heave in the earth millions of years
ago. The boy walks by the rock, rubbing his hands along it, seeming
not to listen. The man walks behind him, looking at his boots, still
talking rather forlornly. He walks carefully because of the camera
swinging from his shoulder, a heavy object, like a box but for the
melodeon lens.

*

MEANWHILE GRANDFATHER IS at home working at his mural, the cost of oils over his latest space having done him out of a week's tobacco. So he works at the breast of Hellas with a bad temper. How does a breast look while a woman is running? He has never encountered the problem before, or a woman like this, statuesque and yet mobile. He pulls his hand back tetchily and the brush scrapes across her jaw. He curses and is about to abandon the brush to its jar of turps when he notices something. The smudge has drawn a shadow across the jaw, lengthened it even, made it what novelists term a lantern jaw. He smiles. He sees a resemblance between his lantern-jawed Hellas and a prominent member of Cummann na mBan. He remembers the puritanism of her public statements. He chuckles, takes out his brush again and with a few strokes completes the likeness. The figure becomes recognisably Irish, a cartoon sharpness about the profile. He stands back and surveys it and feels an odd, delightful surge of power. He returns renewed to her breast, as if the brush is pulling his hand.

*

HIS SON WAS up the Head and his own son beyond him, near the crest. And as James walked, the pace of his steps seemed to match his thoughts. He saw how walking was not a continuum but a series of leaps, how Luke's feet in the distance leapt and landed and leapt again. His own thoughts leapt with them, finding themselves always somewhere else. He thought of how he would die one day and how each moment was a step leading him to that one. He reached the crest and stood there, letting his son run on. He looked at the sea below him, and the bay and he knew suddenly that death was not just like that sea, it was that sea and the only purpose of that sea was to remind him of his death. He felt that if he were to look at death, not death in general, but his private death, if one were to cultivate it like an acquaintance, or like the habit of afternoon tea, one could place all else in relief. There was power and comfort in that thought, of the fact and moment of obliteration cultivated like a friend. His life rose before him, under a garish light. Why, he wondered, why? And the realisation came, shimmering and crimson. In the flash the curate talked about, time, how he had longed to shatter and suppress it and the end of time is death. And how acquaintance with your death would place time between your lips, like a silk ribbon, like a spouse whose mother was already your intimate. To embrace, a conquest and yet an act of love. He threw both of his arms out towards that blanket of sea so that they jerked in their sockets. He gripped it in his arms, that metaphorical sea which the real sea only stood for. It was grey, like when he smelt the eucalyptus and a fine vapour seemed to hover over it, barely there. He stumbled down the Head again. Luke! he shouted, Luke! He ran to where the chairs landed but could see only the ghost of his son below him, tiny, running down the shallow field that led to the first house. He stood there holding the metal pole, the yellow chair swaying above him.

FOUR

SANDYMOUNT, 1928

21

OON RENE WILL appear in an ad in the *Freeman's Journal*, wearing a pair of silk stockings and low-strung shoes. Lili admits herself to be jealous for the first time, really jealous, that is. She is still after all travelling down Trimelston Road each day to the convent school, while her friend's education has come to consist of two years in Miss Conway's school of acting on Clyde Road and whatever treasures she can glean from her increasingly weighty mother who has named herself to the educational authorities as the child's official instructress. This means six-monthly visits from departmental inspectors to their Booterstown house, from which they are absent, for the most part. But when they find mother and child at home, they spend two amazed hours in the company of a thirteen-year-old who is hardly numerate at all, who can repeat Irish words with a wonderful *blas* and intonation but can hardly construct a sentence. She shows herself entranced by large sections of the *Aeneid* and without any of the rules of syntax can make wild and uncannily accurate guesses at the meanings of whole paragraphs. She can barely add, but loves the music of Euclidean geometry.

火

Two fattish gentlemen, each holding briefcases, mid-afternoon in a suburban drawing-room. They sit on couches covered in dust sheets. The curtains are drawn. A light bulb swings from a tasselled shade, compensates for the daylight outside. Mother and daughter seem on the point of departure or arrival, perpetually so. The girl in front of them teases out Pythagoras from the paper they've given her, as if discovering the theorem for the first time. She has crumpled the paper on algebra into a ball. The dark-haired gentleman smokes a cigarette, the fair-haired one a pipe. Signs of irritability seem to threaten their patience. They are used to the national schools, where a teacher would tremble at their every whim, where each class would be a model of discipline and order. But here they are dealing with more than a national school. There have been moves, lately, to re-name the street their office sits on after this girl's father. And different rules, they know, apply to those whose names have some connection with those whose names gave names to streets. So their patience is measured as they watch her grapple with triangles. Until the mother interrupts:

'Give them O'Hussey's *Ode to the Maguire*, dear.'

And Rene stands underneath the amber light and delivers the famous ode. Her voice is unremarkable, but her stance is eloquent. And the bell-like clarity of her words must compensate for her other failings. For the inspectors sigh, with either pleasure or relief, and close their notebooks. Una gives a slight shiver, then asks her again,

'Give them Jacques's speech from *As You Like It*.'

火

BUT THE BEST educations are always through default and Una's determination to instruct her daughter in all the principles of bad acting led, perhaps more than any one thing, to the adult Rene. Una knew by this time that her star was falling and had decided not even to catch it as it came down but to impel her daughter's upwards in its place. She had become resigned at last to the limitations of her talents and the erosion of her public appeal. People no longer said, 'Isn't that so-and-so?' as she passed, forgetting her name but reminded inexorably of a 'somebody' by her flashing black hair and her regal carriage. By now her hair was streaked with grey, her figure was ruined and the clothes she could afford to buy were fairly nondescript. The invitations still came to public ceremonies, but she neglected to attend. For she had gained a sense of humour, a certain delight in incongruity. She laughed when de Valera entered the Dail at last and signed with his left hand over his eyes, and managed to make her Republican friends laugh too. When asked about her late husband she said, 'Yes, Michael,' and gazed towards the west with her old intensity, but realised now that she enjoyed the pose. She came to see, gradually, around her thirty-fifth year, when the only work she could get was in fit-ups touting peasant melodramas round the provinces, that here was a profession and that she belonged to it. She had always mixed political and feigned passion on the stage, been known above all for her 'sincerity', her 'truth' of performance, and she had in fact spoken lines as if not on a stage under lights, in front of flats, but as if in the dusty atmosphere of a nationalist meeting. She had done what all household names do, become an emblem, intruded her real self into the theatrical field and for almost a decade it had sufficed. But then a public, tired with the concerns of her real self and its emblems, had tired of her and she found herself adrift suddenly, in a profession whose mainstay is plain artifice. And she had realised slowly, like a cured invalid learning to use his legs again, the beauty, permanence and humour of the feigned passion. As the last illusion of the *grande dame* left her she found herself among the flotsam of the feigned passion, the permanent hybrids of the profession who keep its laws and pass them on, its humours, its superstitions, its attitudes of wrist, face and hand; the ageing queens, the comedians, the soft-shoe shufflers, the young tap girls, the matrons typecast as such, the outraged suitors, the overbearing parents, the lovers, passionate, true, false and profane: all of them stagestruck. She realised her talent's home and its limitations: these were her people, she was a passable actress, Ireland was a splash of green on a canvas flat. But then, among the profession she had a strange lustre that carried her over her sense of limitation, for they, permanently stagestruck, all remembered her good days. And so she carried the reputation of a once-leading lady the way others did that of a good line in maidservants. And so found herself now, a parody of her former self, playing young heroines in an ageing figure on stages with less than three flats—a parody she enjoyed, revelled in even, carried over with gusto into her real life as slowly, slowly, the balance was reversed and where once she had sinfully pushed the real life on to stage she now extended the rim of the stage to include her boarding-house, her turn of glance in a rural street and all the minutiae of her private life.

⁂

YOU HAD GROWN alongside your mother since that breakfast of butter and sausages in the Killiney hotel when the Republican waiter served you so willingly. You still remember your father's shoulder pistol and his clipped 'Home, Jack' as he lifted you into the open car on the Bray prom. Your life together since he died seemed a process of melting. There are healing graces in human affairs and you have more than your share of them. Through loving you she is reinventing him in a form she can love, expiating her former indifference. Which is perhaps why, when greeted by those who knew all three of you, in the old days, ex-lord mayors of major towns, ex-commanders of guerrilla battalions now heads of government departments, friends of his only, Free-Staters now, friends of hers only, Republicans now, all of those who knew the three of you say, 'How like him she is'. And Una can take this without any rancour. She is even glad of the comparison, she resurrects him in you in a finer form. The part of him that lives through you is after all the mythical part, one simple image of the head framed by the ridiculously large cap and the shoulder pistol. One simple attribute, that of the man of action, distracted, regretful, uneasy with his role. His memory after all has become the embodiment of how different it could have been if only . . . And so when you appear with Una at public functions or at any functions at all and people say how like him you are, they see in you this wonderful, mythical alternative, this possibility of how different it could have been . . . For you are already developing this propensity, this unconscious talent for being seen from any angle and seen differently.

⚜

AT THIRTEEN YOU are fattish and your hair has the same blonde look with the texture of cream that it had when you were six. Your hair and your walk distinguish you, since there's not much that's beautiful in your figure or your face. You smile a lot. There's a lot to smile about for a girl of thirteen with no school to go to. You've adapted yourself to the company of adults since your father died, which could be why your walk is so relaxed. It gives a grace to your figure that shouldn't have been there, belying all the canons of schoolgirl beauty; as if there's a moving centre to you which your figure just follows. You always walk, even in the most high-heeled, the heaviest boots, as if you are barefoot. And all this gives you ease in adult company. You only lose it in the company of your peers, of girls of your age. They are made shy by your habits which, far from seeming adult to them, seem old-fashioned. And the too-adult child always does seem old-fashioned. You have picked up habits of speech and gesture which they associate with their more ardent teachers and the comparison leaves a distance between you and them. You are always polite, for instance, you address a remark to each member of whichever company you are in. You have no sense of exclusiveness, of secrets. You rarely whisper. Your hands are smallish—practical hands that move when you talk using gestures that are never hurried but always startling.

於

RATHER UNGAINLY ADULT clothes, blouses, skirts and dresses of your mother's, which she has taken in. Her sumptuous, evening sense reflected in every garment so you could wear a velvet dress on a spring day, a strange mixture of ill-fitting and style. Your clothes make you suspect to the mothers of those who might possibly be your friends.

So you learn to keep to yourself, you walk down by the stretch of marsh where the birds nest, over the railway line, over the granite ramp to the beach. You are the girl of thirteen with the large eyes and face, the halo of blonde hair, who walks along the railway tracks, stepping on the sleepers. On the beach, among the men in long coats who prod the flotsam with sticks, the young children playing truant from school. There is a woman who holds her belongings in a tied bundle, who sometimes sits by the granite wall. The wall slopes towards the beach, at an angle, to keep the tracks free of spring tides. The children and the lost elders sit there and the occasional sexual predator, generally male. You are the only adolescent girl to grace the granite. The flecks of silver and the mottles of white on the large fawn blocks reflect your hair and your eyes. It is an empty place, though never empty of people. The ramp stretches down the length of the track and yards separate those who sit on it, as if some rule of place keeps them apart; the two children looking through the sea-green bottle at the sun, the man with seven coats asleep in the spring heat, the youth with the ashplant, the high trousers and the slow eyes, following the children and the green bottle. Then there is you. The woman with the bundle intrigues you. She is wearing a grey shawl, like sackcloth. She unties the bundle slowly, unwraps yards of brown paper. You are looking directly at her, something one doesn't do on the ramp and the weekday beach. She takes from the paper an evening dress and a pair of high-heeled shoes and a hat. The hat has mock fruit on top and the sprigs are twisted. The dress is crumpled, though still glittering with sequins. She takes off her shawl, then the garment under that, indistinguishable from her shawl, and lastly a stiff, coarse vest. You can see her withered breasts exposed to the sun as she holds the sequined dress to herself. She has a dowager's hump and the ridges of her spine seem to push through her white skin. She struggles into the sequined dress and pulls it down around waist and thighs, pulling off the cloth she used as a skirt as she does so. Then she puts on the high-heels, dons the hat, turns to you with an unearthly, blissful smile.

'How do they suit me?'

You smile back in answer. You watch her stagger down the ramp, across the sand, towards the sea's edge. She stands there like a thin, twisted bird, the sequins flashing in the sunlight, more sharply than the sea. She is staring at the thread of the horizon, motionless for several minutes, then suddenly she turns and walks back.

'A bit loud, don't you think?'

You are about to reply that you don't think so at all, but you see that she has made up her mind, she's already struggling out of the dress, exposing her thin breasts again. So you smile in affirmation.

火

YOU GIVE THAT sea front your occasional hours round your thirteenth year. The woman with the bundle returns with a different set of garments. Dapper old men wink at you, striding towards Blackrock. You look as odd, perhaps, as most of that ramp's inhabitants, with your handed-down clothes and your air of abstraction, though the thought would never occur to you. Dreaming is a precious thing, at thirteen, on a near-empty beach. Never, I would say, does your mind form one abstract, separated thought. You souse yourself in the mechanics of dreaming, where one thought fades and leads to another and everything turns into everything else. The same breath blows through them, blowing deep, rising to the surface, then deep again. The wind raises a thread of sand and lets it fall. You get up and walk when the mood takes you, following the sand. A man accosts you one morning, a young man, so small and perfect that he could be called dwarf. He smiles at you from the granite. He is impeccably clean, his nails are long and perfectly groomed, his hair runs back from his forehead in thin waves. His small-boned, perfect face has the delicacy of an egg. His lips are tiny, somewhat sad, but his smile breaks his face into tiny creases, exposing even white teeth. He must be amazed when you smile back for he stutters when he calls you to the ramp.

Wait with me, he tells you, for the train. His knees are drawn up and one hand rests on each. It carries an opera singer, he tells you, who will throw roses at anyone who stands and waves. Will you stand and wave? he asks. You walk a little up the ramp so that you can see the tracks. His hands flutter on his knees. Why, you ask him, will she throw out roses? Because she is famous, he tells you, she is famous, most beautiful and has a wonderful voice. If you are quick enough you can catch an armful of them. Red roses, white ones, all colours. Where will I stand? you ask. Here, he says, where she can see you. He stretches up, his small hand touches your thigh. Still, he says. His hand seems to shiver on the velvet. You obey it, don't move. Will you show me your rose, he asks? I have no rose, you tell him, I will have to wait until the train comes. But you have, he insists, flashing his sad lips into a smile. You hear footsteps behind you on the granite and his hand trembles against you. You must watch for the train, he says softly, hastily, a little girl like you. He returns the hand to his knee. When will it come? you ask him, climbing the ramp to the top. Soon, he says, catch me some roses. You see him running backwards across the sand, his neat dwarf's prints before him. Flashing his distant smile. Patience, he cries.

22

THAT IS NOT, however, to be read as your first sexual experience. Nothing but your curiosity was excited, which was perhaps fortunate, and your memory of the miniature man remains with you only because of the whiteness of his teeth and the neatness of his cuticles. You thought of nothing more significant than the train and the roses when he'd left you. The machine of adolescence had to wait to come, and the train with it.

It needed Lili to meet you on the straw-coloured ramp, to cross the sand to the sea and back again. Lili comes in the more normal hours, the afternoon hours, when the place has lost its emptiness. There are comparative crowds then, schoolgirls, like Lili, in uniform. You walk down the tracks, you clamber over the sleepers, she holds your hand with one hand, presses down her blowing skirt with the other. She hints at that machine of the age beyond reason. You feel the world of intimacies, whispers and fluttering eyes. You are surprised and embarrassed since your world of adults has kept you a child, strangely innocent, innocently mature. You have stayed blissfully unaware of these long secrets of girlhood, which Lili seems to want to share. A blush, deep and rose-coloured, a sense of shame that she should be shamed, rises on your cheek, which makes Lili giggle and makes you blush more. The blush seeps inside, it becomes a positive warmth. 'Scarlet, like a rose,' says Lili, alluding to your cheeks and perhaps your hands do go to cover your face since her air of classroom banter increases your discomfort. You feel that this sensation welling inside you as you cover the tracks, manifesting itself in your cheeks in this glorious red, is one that deserves to be talked of in more than whispers. It should be discussed, you feel, with more elaborate manners than those of the diplomatic banquet your mother once brought you to. Or it should be shouted from high places, from the windows of trains, bringing roses to places you have never heard of. You cross from the tracks and climb up on the ramp and begin to tell Lili of your miniature man. But Lili tugs your palm, whispers that you should keep your voice down. A nun is passing, and the ramp is too narrow for three. You stand with your back to the sea to allow her walk by, tall, boxed and birdlike. You recognise the face beneath the bonnet, the greying hair. You call her name, though Lili's hand goes out to stop you. And Sister Paul turns, her face changing from puzzlement to recognition to the quick smile that you remember so well, creasing the translucent skin. As she talks above the railway tracks in a voice hardly different from the one in which she introduced you to the age of reason you wonder what her name would be for this new age, the one Lili seems to hold between her lips now, like a mouthful of shamed peach. It is an age, you sense, containing truths so immense that only a discipline like hers could do it justice. Behind you the tide seeps from the creases of sand.

火

YOU CAME OF age on a day in July. It was a Monday and the beach was wholly deserted. One nun passed, whom you looked at closely, hoping to see Sister Paul's smile. But it was a plumper face, buried under the folds of a different habit. The blocks of the ramp were so hot that you could hardly sit. You sat, though, and let their heat change into a private warmth. The tide was higher than you'd ever known it, halfway up the granite, obscuring the beach. You lay for hours in the swoon of that heat, your cheek touching the granite so that your eye travelled down from the tan of the stone, so hot that its surface seemed to dance, to the huge, perfect blue world of that sea. You knew something was happening, that time was longer than it should have been and you allowed those minutes to pass like hours, teasing every fragment of yourself out into the sensual glare of that surface. You imagined bubbles you had to burst repeatedly to find further bubbles inside them, you laid one cheek on the granite and then the other so that the sea seemed to leave its fixed position and globe above you, around you. There was a slight tremor in the granite and you sensed a train far off. You saw a tanker inching across the horizon and then the ground moved beneath you, every pore in the granite seeming to leap to your cheek and the train, going where, you wondered, came and was gone. You imagined the tide, higher than it ever should have been, flooding the ramp, water spilling over the granite on to the sleepers and tracks.

23

WOULD SHE ALWAYS connect orgasm with trains, the even sleepers stretching into the distance and the border of black rail, meeting somewhere beyond her vision where they melted in a dance of haze, or in perfect union, where the laws of perspective told her they could never meet, only appear to? Or with the train itself, the mysterious rumble in the turf causing twigs to leap, heralding the sight through the haze of distance of 'the one friendly machine'? She called it that later, when she spent more hours on it than off it. But the convivial machine roars past and the child waves and never knows whether her wave is received by the unknown face in that strip of windows, whether the memory is carried towards a far-off station, a platform, a black footbridge. And the hope of roses always, for the pure-hearted waver. She would wave her hand years later, like the child who rarely sees trains. She would think of roses blooming from the window, sprouting from the axles. She would picture the landscape towards which the train always goes, always a foreign one, a garish plain where the tracks run over pliant peat, pass a disused canal and enter a clump of fir trees. The fir trees dip in gratitude. It is the landscape into which she has never been, towards which the train heads as it thunders past her, always beyond the farthest town, never on maps. She walks along the tracks looking for that carriage the dwarf told her of, which is small, like a childhood train. The tracks pass the canal that is now solid with frogspawn which falls over the sides of its banks, clinging to the fringe of pebbles by the track's edge. It spawns even as she walks. It clings to her bare feet like the gossamer of snails and she runs lightly to avoid it, stepping from sleeper to sleeper, between the tracks. The wood of those sleepers has fallen soft with age and holds the print of each of her steps. The tracks are bright with their oxides, a glare of red she never thought rust could achieve, and they thread the crest of the bog, towards the fir trees. She is walking with her head down, following the tracks and yet not following, for each sleeper is an end in itself and with each step she takes she knows she has come. The function of tracks is to lead the train from one point to another and the tracks themselves she knows are neither arrival nor departure, just partaking a little of both. But the soft wood of the sleepers and the frogspawn always doubling itself tells her with every footfall that she is here. And seen from behind, she knows, her walk would always intimate arrival, a bundle of static moments somehow thrown through time. You are here, the tracks say to her, and she holds this message as she would a towel to her bare breasts, her head bent downwards, knowing that somewhere beyond her the tracks do indeed meet. She feels the slightest shift of her thoughts could destroy this and so she walks with a terror, a terror that she feels necessary to maintain her sense of joy. For through this landscape in which every point is the point of arrival and every step is the ultimate step, she cannot deny that she is walking and that these tracks do lead towards that clump of fir trees and pass through it, to beyond. The frogspawn leaps as if to celebrate her thoughts and rises in imitation of the fir trees until she is among them and a soft glove of pine needles covers the tracks. She is at the point, she sees, where the sides of the tracks meet, despite all the laws of perspective. And beyond where the tracks seam into one lies the train the little man told her of, glorious and aged. There is that bright red which rust could hardly manage. But it is rust, she sees as she draws nearer, a kind of passionate rust for the metal surface falls apart at her touch into puffs of the russet. And the rust seems there to high-light the forgotten roses. They spill from every crevice of the body-work, from underneath the axle, from the cracks in the leather of the passenger seats. They are red and she is bathed in their shadow. She walks to the driver's cabin, through the brambles.

火

I HAVE PLACED the train with the roses by a disused canal and a clump of fir trees in the Bog of Allen, a flat open plane which is tra-versed by rail tracks, a wasteland between town and city. You tell it to Lili on the same ramp several days later. Your face flushes, but without a hint of coyness. You revere the physical details, moreover, the gleams of mica, the bumps of granite, the heat. Lili squirms and even now squirms before me in the telling, 'Because I was a school-girl, yes, I may as well admit it, but there was more than that. I mean I feared for her. I sensed, you see, that my shyness was given to me, my bashfulness was learnt along with my history lessons and that was how it was, a bashfulness that, whether you like it or not, is safer and much more common than forthrightness. And if Rene hadn't learnt it—not only that, she wouldn't learn it, her reaction to every giggle of mine made me feel inconsequential, worse than a child, a retarded adult—what would happen to her when she had to confront the source of that bashfulness? If she was extraordinarily lucky, she would never have to confront it, but how many of us are that lucky? And I feared for her, you see, and that's why I blushed— or that's as much why I blushed as my shame was why, if you know what I mean. And I was right to fear and blush, I discovered, when she told me that extraordinary story about the dwarf. And then I was made conscious of the fact—as she was never—the fact that we were both thirteen. Only thirteen. And that in many ways I was older than her . . . would she ever pass thirteen . . . and so I blushed and feared for . . .'

火

THEY EXCHANGE THESE confidences on the hottest days the beach has encountered, two girls, sitting on the lip of the ramp. Trains pass occasionally with the speed of a long, slow exhalation. The granite dances in the haze that makes the beach's inhabitants seem removed, far-off, transfixed against the blue sky and the yellow sand. But both girls hardly notice them. They are inside the bubble of their own warmth, their own words. Lili is reminded of that day the class exchanged confessions, of the rows of desks, the irises. Rene is talking, using words that are too young and too old for her thirteen-year-old mouth. She has her legs drawn into her chin, her hands are clutching her calves, damp with perspiration. Her legs are plumpish, Lili swears. Three years later they will be on the back page of the *Freeman's Journal*. They will have slimmed by then, be still fairly short, but give a definite impression of adulthood.

✵

'BUT THE YEARS passed like days on that ramp. And when we finally got up with our bums creased with all that granite, it was three years later. She was sixteen—'

24

WHILE LUKE VANCE and James stand waiting at Bray station, part of the line caves in on the way to Greystones. A wave that must have germinated far out rises like an open hand, clutches the tracks and drags them towards itself. The metal bends in the water and the sleepers scud through the foam, haloed by the spray. The Bray train knows nothing of this but exhales a welcoming shroud of steam to them, father and son. Luke carries the tripod, James the case. They walk through the steam, through the door and take their seats on the seaward side.

⚹

'SHE HAD A premonition, I suppose. The dark wings brushed off her, making her cloaks flap. You will be a professional, she told Rene, there is a photographer I know. I came with them. It will be your assignment, she told her, your money. I walked with them down O'Connell Street. Can you imagine that voluminous animal dying, being there one moment, gone the next? I can't, even now. I had lived her through her stories, secondhand ever since I'd known them. But did she know, I often wonder, was that photograph a hint that she

would someday live in Rene, Rene alone? An acquaintance stopped
her on O'Connell Bridge. They talked for a while, they had that tone
of voice, as when you talk of the Free State—'

⚰

BUT WHAT IS it that delights Una as she walks towards the agency
with both of them beside her? It comes to her in an unfathomable shift,
a sudden, unheralded flood of happiness. She has grown heavier, but
she now holds her weight like a flag, a proud flag of she knows not
what nation, an imposing black cloak thrown round her shoulders
fluttering with the sea breeze that meets them on the bridge. The salt
brings a flush to her cheeks as it had when she walked towards that
spa, past the fluttering canvas, sixteen years earlier. She knows now
that she loves this street with its giant pots and its green litter bins
and its aura of sea coursing through it, keeping all those flags that
crowd the rooftops jerking as if they themselves remember the course
of events that put them there. The only faces that turn as they walk
are those surprised by the unlikely aspect of this trio and she accepts
the stares with equanimity, knowing that at last they are directed not
at herself but at the daughter to her left whom she guides through the
afternoon crowds like a statue, a more perfect image of herself. The
wide, lengthy street seems a unit to her, an image of temporal home,
and homes, she knows, are for leaving. A man steps from the crowd
to catch her attention and the wind flaps his fawn overcoat as it does
her cloak. He talks to her like an intimate and she hardly bothers
to recognise him. He talks of the state and the arms dumps. They
will be there, he tells her, waiting to be resurrected should Dev take

one step backwards. She remembers the old complicity, the common words and gestures, the nods of emphasis for certain names, of negation for others. He is reviving, he tells her, the Conradh classes in Parnell Square. He asks her to lend a hand. She nods, as he assumes she will, and she feels a hidden surge of delight at his mistaken assumption. She sees herself and her large cloak and the person she has always seemed facing him and another impulse makes her turn and continue her walk down that wide street thinking of everything that seems, of people in groups and nods of assent and flags jerking gracelessly from rooftops. She passes the General Post Office with its three females pointing heavenwards and the wide, wide street with its flapping banners stretches out before her as if the bricks had been laid, demolished and laid again, as if the bullet holes had scarred the angels' feet just so that she could walk finally down it, closing her hand around her daughter's elbow and lead her towards her first professional assignment.

火

'SHE WAS MORE real than she ever had been. We walked up two flights of stairs into a room that was painted black. A man put the silk stockings on Rene. He sat her on a podium in different positions. Then the door was pushed ajar in a way that was irritating, hesitant. And I saw him coming through it for the first time. Was it the door that irritated me or was it him? I can't distinguish. And the boy Luke came behind him carrying the tripod. Chalk and cheese.'

火

LUKE STARES AT the legs of Rene. He wants to touch them, even then. Which of them, father or son, can I choose? James shakes hands with the voluminous Una and speaks to her in broken Irish. He looks towards her daughter through the dust of the arc lamp, rubbing his eyes. The man smooths the silk stockings.

⚱

'SHE WOULDN'T LIVE to see her daughter's picture. We walked back down the street towards the G.P.O. and she held my arm so tight that it hurt. I turned to ask her to loosen it and I saw all the colour had gone from her face. I walked on. I was puzzled. Each of us is alone.'

⚱

THE WIND GATHERS far out in the bay, up the estuary to the bridge and coils down the street like a silk ribbon. It whips Una's skirts like a flag, she stands still, they wait for her to move again. It whips each fragment of her past into a gale, would lift her over the parapet and the angel's feet and the tips of the marble spears, make each memory sweet, each enemy a loved one. It smells of the sea, the divine pungency of salt, would lift her only to dissolve her. They wait outside the G.P.O. until she gathers enough strength to walk on.

⚱

'BUT NOBODY DIES,' Lili whispered, 'and now you're bringing her to life again. She just left a voluminous emptiness in the Pro-Cathedral.

It was emptier for all those who didn't attend. Where were they all, I wondered, from the great days? There was no mention in the papers, no photograph even. De Valera was represented by a mass-card. I sat with Rene in the pews, among the actors. We had the same black veils. James came up, without his black box this time. If there's anything I can do to help, he said. There would be something, though that would come later. Luke stood behind him, staring. I turned to see what he was staring at. It was the silk stockings, of course, which she had never taken off—'

25

I F THERE'S ANYTHING I can do—James asked her on the Pro-Cathedral steps. And as Lili said, there would be. But did he search her out or did he wait for chance to tell him to search her out? The one event occurred that made a pattern of all the other events and without that event, he must have thought, months later, all the events before it would have been random. But the event occurred and took the others, like stringless beads, pulling a sudden thread through them. So afterwards he can muse in retrospect, on Killiney Head, always his incessant walks, kicking the cones away with his high-laced boots, how each must have held the germ of the significance with which it was later blessed. And so that photograph in the Green Room led to the next in the O'Connell Street dark room, each one gaining in portent with the one that followed. And the equations lovers tease themselves with—if A had not happened, then B would never have been possible, if we had never met there, we would never—he developed gradually into a mathematics of chance, passion and happenstance. We are all small nations, he would tell her later, and our past, present and future is a moving thread. And so he had photographed her twice when he met her the third time, and the circumstances of that meeting made him clutch, for the first time, at the thread. There were flowers on the altar again, funereal ones, and the priest moved with his waxen gestures against the backdrop of the cross. He looked around him and saw actors he recognised, some of whom recognised him. He felt a slight puzzlement at the sense of occasion, even at his presence there. She had never appealed to him when alive, as an actress even, and yet dead she seemed to unite these few mourners with a sense of larger event. He remembered her husband's death and the whole streets with covered windows. Time, as it lengthens, magnifies its figures, where distance miniaturises. Where are the soldiers, he wondered, looking around him for medals strung to lapels, where are the politicians? Have all the great events happened? And yet she was larger, somehow, for their absence. Every actor there he'd photographed at one time or another. Lord, he almost prayed, open my lips. And then he saw her daughter from behind, centre of the event, the blonde hair threading through the black lace veil. He felt that the mother had left so that the daughter could be seen more clearly. He let his eyes travel upwards from her blonde and lace threads to the huge dome above, the two lesser ones on either side. He thought of a dome where each brick is the cornerstone. When his eyes travelled down again through the pantheon of saints on the wall below he saw that the mourners had risen and the actors were walking out behind her. He followed them to the steps outside and it was there, with the wind blowing down Marlborough Street, tugging at everyone's dark clothes, that he asked was there anything he could do.

火

THERE WOULD, AS Lili said, be something he could do. He saw the print with the silk stockings in the daily papers. The brand turns out to be popular. It's the girl we photographed, isn't it? Luke asks him, lifting the newspaper from the green-topped table. He nods, wondering vaguely why his son uses the plural. You must learn to use the camera, he tells Luke, who shakes his head, always uninterested. You must learn Irish then. Why? Luke asks. You must do everything, he tells him. You must succeed where I failed. He looks at his son's profile, half-lit through the grey window. Luke is tearing the print from the page. Listen, he says, you must listen. Why, Father? Luke asks, his face made translucent by the grey metal light. You are my beloved son, he says, you must be everything I am not. But you made me, Luke says, turning his face around to the light. Luke shows the cut-out square of print to the old man, who proclaims it a masterful knee. I won't be with you much longer, the old man says, standing in the doorway. For a little while, then I won't be with you. You are my father, James says, you will always be with us. You made me. You made me, says Luke, turning again from the light. The old man shuffles back upstairs to where he mixes his pigments. Up there he dreams of them both, with his shock of white hair. James walks around the table to Luke until they are both washed in the light. He takes the paper from his son's hands.

火

SOMEWHERE IN THE mass of print that swims around the space where her knees were, there is an announcement, in the curt phrases of exhibition notices, of a benefit concert for Rene O'Shaughnessy, daughter of Una. He meets her there of course, having taken the Bray train and seen the eucalypti from below, bare in the twilight, dipping hugely from the summit towards the sea. It is a sad enough affair in a governmental hall with rows of tubular steel chairs half-empty, a wooden seat and wooden back to each. A succession of artistes take the bright-lit stage and preface each act with a few words in remembrance. He listens to the tenor voices, the duos and trios, the recitations, the scraps from Boucicault and Synge. A sense of pity floods over him, whether for himself or her he can't be sure. He watches a much younger Lili recite 'My Dark Rosaleen' and approaches Rene in the interval, flooded as always with kindness. Lili drinks tea and eats a damp biscuit and begins to learn her impatience with him. A man in a check jacket, whom Rene calls Brogan, hands her a cheque. Is it coincidence, he asks Rene, that I took two photographs of you, each one near a death? She must have smiled. You could teach my child Irish, he says, embarrassed by his impulse, if you're in need of work. Your mother I remember had a *blas*. He stumbles with the unlikely word. She smiles, watching his lips quiver. But of course, he said, you act—

꽃

DURING THE SECOND half he finds himself beside her. A man called MacAllister proclaims her talents from the stage. Something in the man's air irritates him. The words are too pat, the phrases too ritual, she deserves more than this paternal show of warmth. She seems everyone's favourite, though. She sits upright, like a child in class, dutifully looking towards that cone of light. When he turns he can see the tip of her profile, behind the fringe of hair. The outer strands could brush his lips. She has one leg crossing the other.

26

'FOR SHAPELIER LEGS' says the caption. The contrasts are hard, as his gaze must have been. Rene's calf swells from that phrase in a long arc away from the ankle-strap. A seam traces the line of her calf and disappears into the upper of a high-heeled shoe. Her other leg juts from the lower left-hand corner, to be crossed by the first, the one that fills the picture. This leg seems pliant, resting but not at rest, as if with a benign and wholly female tolerance of time it had been swinging for an afternoon and just stopped for the shutter to click.

FIVE

BRAY, 1933

27

L ARGE HOUSES AREN'T in demand these days and so when I went to Number One Sydenham Villas at the time the auctioneer had mentioned, I found it empty. The door was half-open; it was daylight outside but not a voice came through that strip of shade. The villas stretched up to my right, none as big as the first. It had been built, I imagine, when there was nothing there but field, one imposing building on the outskirts of a miniature Bray. The street and the rest came later, each year another and a smaller house, shrinking through the decades, adopting a perspective as if time were trying to imitate space. I inched the door open and watched the strip of shadow grow. The sea boomed from the prom. I felt proud of these dimensions. Nothing smaller would have done you, father or grandfather, whichever you turn out to be. I stepped inside and I smelt his world, knowing each detail was right whether it happened or not, each fact was part of him, whether real or not. There was the hatstand with the ball-and-claw feet. My shoulder touched the door, which touched it. The feet tottered and the four whorled handles swayed. I stood there, watching it totter. The hall stretched out in front of me. There were two doors off it to the left. The wall where the old man's mural should have been was covered in paper with an orange and green rose pattern, stretching up the stairs. It was soothing, even beautiful

to stand there with the hatstand banging against the door and the
breeze coming in from the prom below. I felt at home in the only
home there is, that of imagination verified. I walked slowly through
the hall and into a large kitchen, the one room I hadn't catered for.
I had quite forgotten the necessity of making meals and the fact that
these three males would never have done so themselves, would have
needed maidservant, char and cook. There was a range covered with
a film of dust. But you can't put in everything, I thought, though
Luke must have sat curled up there for hours, dreaming in the heat.
I went out to the hall again and into the front room and there was
a bay window with a circular sofa and a piano against the left-hand
wall. There was no green felt-topped table. But it could have been
removed years ago, and besides, Lili gave me that piece. I felt the
floor beneath me, the walls around me, the house, valued at £30,000
in the auctioneer's brochure, needing repairs, the whole magnificence
of fact. And the repairs would have been extensive. There were dark
patches on the cream walls and the plaster bubbled from the ceiling
and as I walked towards the bay window one of the floorboards gave
way under my shoe. There was just the skeleton of how they lived
there, overlaid perhaps with the décor and the knick-knacks of three
generations, layers of paint and sheaves of wallpaper, decades deep.
But when I lay down on the circular sofa and rested my elbow on
the curved sill and stretched my legs along the damp felt I could have
peeled away those generations with my eyes and left the walls the
way they were then, a thin blue, I would imagine, or perhaps the pal-
est of greens. I could see the white horses beyond the promenade and
the long trail of a jet, dissolving as the daylight went. And the nose
of Bray Head edged past the window, rippled and frozen in the curve

of the glass. The yellow pylons were still there, and the wooden café at the top where the passengers of the chair-lift used to alight, but the yellow chairs were gone and so the cables swung now, weightless. Why are the earliest photographs touched with an irresistible melancholy and why do the faces of loved ones we never met seem as large as the prints themselves are tiny? Did everyone feel more then?

I rose from the bay window and walked back across the room. I could have been walking on a beach, placing my feet in a trail of footprints much larger than mine. It took me years to cross from bay window to door, so huge had the room become. Halfway there I heard the front door bang. The hatstand rocked again, in counterpoint to someone's footsteps. I reached the door and opened it quietly, so as not to startle a prospective buyer. I saw a figure with slightly bowed shoulders and a neck which must once have been sleek and plump but from which the flesh hung limply now like those stiff folds of cloth in ecclesiastical murals. He was wearing a black hat, flecked round the rim. He was staring at the far wall, much as I had done earlier. I spoke without thinking.

'Can the paint have survived the wallpaper?'

※

IT WAS INDEED the curate. He turned, not at all surprised, smiling faintly. He had aged, of course, from when I had imagined him. There were forty more years, with the thirty-one I'd given him. That he drank I could see from his face, but his eyes had stayed bright in the interval, alert with his passion for theology and maths. Had his hope survived, I wondered, not without a twinge of conscience, had he unified those disciplines I'd given him so rashly? He spoke then and I thought, yes and no.

'Will we investigate?'

His voice seemed to come from an extraordinary depth, roughened by the layers of dust it had to shake off to reach me. Most of his teeth were gone. His eyes brightened with a humorous twinkle as he reached one hand up, gripped a sagging corner of the wallpaper and ripped one strip away. We both stood back and stared at the Hellenic form, head, neck and shoulders revealed above the jagged edge. It was the face of a woman with those stiff, airborne curls, her head turned in profile, looking with benign curiosity at something hidden by the wallpaper roses. Her halo of hair, her neck and her beautiful muscular shoulders were suspended, superimposed almost, over a landscape of low grey hills, Hellenic or Hibernian I couldn't have said. The curves and definition of those hills looked suspiciously like the background to Leonardo's 'Virgin of the Rocks', but the woman's face was all the old man's own; vibrant and childlike, primitive or kitsch, I couldn't have cared less since it spoke to me. I have never made aesthetic judgments.

'He mixed his own paints, you see.'

The colours were still fresh where the plaster had bubbled with damp. They were spread thinly, evenly, with nowhere the mark of a brushstroke, as if he wanted to disguise the nature of his materials. It gave his colours the worst possible texture, the texture of a photograph, a photograph of beings who were somehow larger, whose poses were more deliberate than the landscape spread out before them; of a being, too, who had attained the grandeur of colour when the world was being photographed in black and white.

✹

OUR THOUGHTS WERE interrupted by the door opening again and banging against the hatstand and the entry of two well-heeled families, everyone clutching the auctioneer's brochure. We turned abruptly from the torn wallpaper as if to dispel any possible connection between us and it and I sensed, gratefully, that we had in common a mutual feeling of guilt. His was complicated by an added factor, however, since both families, despite the profanity of their staring open-mouthed at the torn wallpaper without noticing the mural, all turned to him and smiled as we walked towards the door, repeating among themselves the word 'Father'. This embarrassed him, I am glad to say, as much as it incensed me and so when we reached the open door and the view of the night sea I felt a positive bond between us. He placed his hand on my elbow as I'm sure he did to Luke, as I'm sure he did to all three of them, at first to steady himself as we went down the steps but then to confide in me, as we made our way out of the gate, with the warmth in his palm and his voice of what I felt for an instant must be a much younger man.

28

'I DIDN'T KNOW HER,' he said when the wind hit us, 'but I assume it must be her. Yes, although I've never seen her I've imagined her just like that. Luke described her once across the grille, a bizarre confession, but then all confessions are bizarre, there's just the pleasure of listening, a refined pleasure, let me tell you and one that has to be nurtured. As a young priest it used to terrify me, I used to slide back the hatch at any opportunity I got, would you believe, just to let my face be seen and if possible to get a glimpse at whoever was muttering the words but of course that was just a palliative, there was no cure was what I had to realise, people ceased to come to me for after all the sinner demands and deserves the right to whisper unseen. And the only way to live with the objects of one's terror after all is to take pleasure in them, which is what I had to do. Listening sets the imagination relatively free, you see, on a leash with a hand guiding it. But there was a whole country at it then, with radios, villages would gather in the bicycle shops to hear the Saturday match and so it was a confessional state, you see, in its early days, in more ways than one since everyone had their ear bent to a speaker. And so I—'

He stopped and I felt his hand on my arm again.

'Will we walk round by the Head?'

I nodded and we turned and walked back down the prom.

'And so I, instead of building a blow-by-blow account of the hurls on Croke Park from a cracked speaker, built a picture of her from a year of rumours, from one confused confidence of Luke's and even from my philosophic discussions with James, God bless his heart, since though he never mentioned her name, his thought around that time became somehow more inclusive. She was plumper, I may tell you, in my mind's eye, plumper than we have just seen her on that wall but that, I suppose, could be attributed to the old man's faulty vision. I have seen him on the prom here, on that patch of grass which used to be bald from his stool and easel, staring at the Irish Sea and yet something more akin to the Mediterranean appearing on his canvas. But I have no doubt, have you, that what we have just seen is her—'

I had no doubt. She had an adaptable figure, Lili had told me.

'I visited the house for years before she came, and the year she came my visits stopped. It was a house without a mother, you see, and in a sense it was waiting for her, and perhaps that's why my visits had to stop. If you detect a hoarseness in my voice it is because I am close to tears even now, thinking of it. Yes, I did look forward to those visits, to tea and cucumber sandwiches and to Luke taking out the tray. James and I talked mathematics and theology, we compared notes from the current journals, he stopped taking instruction after the first year, but that didn't matter. What mattered I suppose was a young curate walking from a presbytery to this household on the Bray prom and the light coming in from the bay window. Or did that matter? Our arguments were extraordinarily intense. We would hold positions for weeks on end and then drop

them suddenly on a whim, because of the weather or the colour of
the bay outside. James retained a fundamentalist frame of mind,
you see, despite his agnosticism, he brought an intellectual rigour
to the examination of the new state to which that state could never
conform. A sense of chaos however is endemic to Catholic thought
and a very definite mistrust of the intellect, and that of course was
endemic to me, no matter how bad a priest I later became. And so
we faced each other over the gulf of our background, I could see
the weeping Huguenot in him, the personage his father had lost but
which must have been reborn in him by proxy as it were, from perhaps his father's father, for likenesses I have always noticed recur
across two generations, rarely one. And so through the years I lived
his various schemes with him, you have heard about his schemes
no doubt. He allied himself to A.E.'s agricultural movement at one
stage, at another he bought that school in Connemara to show the
Bray slum youth the west of Ireland, and later he made a foray into
politics—what was it his brochure said—'to draw the current Irish
dialogue into a European framework'. Of course he lost his de-
posit, a two hundred pounds which he could ill afford, but perhaps
that was better, since we all know what happened to the European
framework for the current dialogue. In fact I am tempted to say
that it was better that all his schemes failed, schemes like his should
fail, since the execution of them could never approach the delight of
their conception and their failure at least allowed him to continue
scheming, which the success of any one of them would have pre-
cluded. And he returned each time, of course, to his abstract art, the
one we shared, mathematics, and the one that both consumed and
fed him, photography.

'So you can imagine how much I loved that house with its cucumber sandwiches, "cues" I see they are called now in the vegetable
shops, and its three generations of males and perhaps it was the fact
that there was no woman there that enabled me to call so often. You
see, once June began my visits had to stop since the Vance family,
minus grandfather of course, would take off on holiday, not your
two-week holiday, but generally two to three months in the country. Of course there were invitations to visit whatever small house
they had rented along the western seabord but I never took them up,
no, holidays for me were at the open centre in Carnsore Point, any
request to visit a whimsical Protestant family in the west of Ireland
would have definitely been suspect. Was it this we shared, I wonder,
this absence of femininity, because it often seemed that all our discussions in that sagging house concerned an absence which all three
of them suspected might one day be filled. James's distance, the old
man's brusqueness when he saw me and the day I sat in the wooden
box in the church on Main Street and this figure stumbled in and
talked hoarsely in a voice that was trying to disguise itself but that I
recognised as Luke's, they all added up to—'

火

WE HAD COME to the end of the promenade tiles and the beginning
of the cement path that still led along the sea but that had fields now
to its left and moved upwards towards the Head. There were chunks
of rock and pebbles set in the cement and he held my arm again as
we walked.

火

'THEY ALL ADDED up to not so much a figure but the impression one has of a figure when it—she in this case—has left the room. The smell of scent perhaps, the cigarette stubbed out on the ashtray— though of course she didn't smoke—a certain mustiness in the case of women which I as a celibate am peculiarly alive to, hanging round a chair, and above all the attitude on people's faces, the look of delayed surprise, affection or fear, retaining as they do the expressions with which they gazed on her even after she has left. Now all the words passed between us in those years, the small tensions, James's elbow, which I often grasped when excited, and good Lord, I did get excited at times, the hand with which I used to pat Luke's head when she eventually did come, in 1933, and my visits stopped—of my own accord, let me hasten to impress on you—James implored me to visit again, but I knew it was finished, we both knew and what contact I did have with them was in my presbytery or on the steps of the church or now and then on the Dublin train—when she eventually did come I could see as clearly as, if you will allow me the simile, Augustine saw his city of God, I could see that all those points in our contact over the years were signs, hints if you like, about her. And that is why when we stood in the hallway just now and I ripped back the wallpaper, I could tell that the figure painted there was her, I could say quite truthfully that I recognised her. Though as I said to you, I would have thought of her as plumper—'

火

WE HAD BY now come to the end of the cement walk and we turned
as if with one mind and walked across the fields, upwards. We came
to where the pylons for the chair-lift were and stopped. I stared up
at the empty cables.

✹

'WE DID WELL to leave that house, for how can you confine it to an
auctioneer's brochure or price it at thirty thousand? Better to let it
fall down, don't you think, decay in its own time, let the roof fall in
and the plaster bulge and peel off the walls? But things aren't let die,
are they, they're bought again and redecorated, shoved into life once
more to house other families, give birth to new memories in turn,
there'll be a television where the circular sofa was and maybe an electric cooker in place of the range, all to house new myths that people
think will die as they do and if they were to return like us they'd be
appalled to find the resilience of objects and the indestructibility of
life, to learn that the end was in the beginning even as it happened,
and the beginning in the end. And even that cable that you're staring
at will carry another yellow chair—'

✹

AND SURE ENOUGH the cable creaked as I was looking at it and
began to roll. I could see the grease glistening in the moonlight and
a yellow chair passed over us, swaying towards the wooden café at
the top. It was approaching summer, I surmised, and some Bray businessman had revitalised the lift.

29

THE FIRST THING Rene would have noticed coming down the Bray prom would have been that lift. She has just come off the train and the directions the photographer scrawled out for her lead back past the station, over the tracks and down towards the sea front. The promenade before her is a mile and a half long, narrowing, it seems, towards this mass of green, neither hill nor mountain, shouldering a gaunt half-circle into the blue sea. And the yellow chairs are moving up and down the Head again. And what crowds on the prom, in the heat, in the middle of summer! She makes her way between them, wearing another pair of silk stockings and of high-heeled shoes. The heels are slightly lower now but still sharp enough to catch in the gaps between the tiles. So she throws her weight forward to the balls of her feet, walking in the way she would if she were barefoot. There are the awnings of the hotels and the porches, some makeshift for the summer, all of striped canvas; the façades of the hotels all facing the beach with the striped deckchairs and the circular canvas tents. Ireland in the heat is a different country, she told herself, imagining boxes with palms bound around with hoops. She changes her pace to avoid the flow coming towards her, but keeps her eyes on the yellow chairs. They go up the Head in jerks, swaying as they move. Her father held her on the yellow chair, showing her the vista. Home, Jack, he said, down the promenade. The voices around her are Scottish now, for the cycle has begun. Heat in summer makes the strollers seem to dance, raises their feet above the surface, blurs the tiled promenade. Perhaps they saw her walking on air, as she saw them, inches above the melting tiles. Or are Scots naturally incurious? The curate certainly doesn't see her, though she sees him. A figure in black on such a hot day stands out. Walking quickly, from what he doesn't yet know will be his last afternoon discourse. She smiles when she sees him; turns, hoping to catch his attention. She is as demure as with Sister Paul, wants to meet all kinds of religious. But Father Beausang's head is full of Descartes, sweltering inside his circular stove, for it's on that appropriate theme that their talks have ended. He senses an ending as he walks, and he is not sure why. Is it the sea, blurred and distended in the heat to abolish the horizon? But he hardly notices the sea. Perhaps it is his suit, which as he walks has covered his body in a film of sweat. The figures that come towards him on the promenade seem to dance in the heat. As he claimed, after she had come, it was as if he knew all along she or something like her would. And so he must sense the ending. And passing the young woman who has smiled at him with an invitation to stop, he just sees another melting figure among the strollers coming towards him and wishes the heat, anyway, would end. And she turns, after a moment standing still, looking after his figure under its creased hat, which soon melts like the other strollers. She walks on to where the hotels give way to residential houses. She stops outside the largest of them, takes her eyes from the yellow chairs and walks in.

火

JAMES VANCE OPENS the door. He sees her standing, framed by the doorway as in both of his prints. But now the sea is behind her and she is a woman. She is shifting her weight from foot to foot too, as the girl in his prints could never have done. He sees her shoes and silk stockings, like the ones he photographed, their silk perfection vanishing under a very imperfect, even shabby, skirt. She has been doing more adverts, he thinks. Perhaps he wishes she could be held static like the girl he photographed, for when she moves into the hallway to stand beside him, he stays looking at the frame of the door. The sun comes in round its edges, bleaching the sea. He will later remember how glad he was, and how ashamed to be glad, that Father Beausang had left.

He says, Come in, which is unnecessary, since she is already in, staring at the extraordinary scene that covers half the wall. He stands at the open doorway watching her against that scene, thinking how her features blend with it. The old man, sensing something, clatters from his attic to the top of the stairs and gazes at her distracted, thinking the woman of his imagination, coaxed by his mural, has at last come alive. And Luke comes from the living-room with the tea things. He is now sixteen.

30

A T FIRST SHE taught her brand of Irish at weekends but she must have felt immediately at home there, for she soon comes to flood the album, and all the vistas that were photographed without her find themselves in print again, with her in the foreground and Luke or James behind. Some rustic fencing with its border of roses which must have bloomed that summer acts as a frame for her, with Luke leaning sullenly against one of the poles and her hand on his sixteen-year-old head. And the old man finds his way in too, finally, magnificently. He is standing bolt upright on the prom, his huge white mane with a sharp quiff at the parting, from which all their quiffs sprang. He has her arm firm through his arm and is clutching it proudly, as if she were his young wife. The Head can be seen behind them and the yellow chairs, which in the print show like puffs of fawn. I can see them having walked the length of the prom, the breezes from the east that came in waves lifting his mane of hair and the hem of her skirt. She has constantly to hold down her skirt, which fills with wind, billowing like a canvas tent, while the old man entertains her with his version of time lost, tells her about the Barbados, about boarding-houses in New York and about the yards and yards of canvas he has filled with paint. Every memory recalls a bad canvas and as he recounts it it seems he dispenses with it, clears

himself of the burden of looking once and for all. He shows her the
bald patch of lawn where he has sat sporadically throughout the last
six years, painting the scene through which he is now walking, a
scene that never seemed as perfect as it is today, and as he says that
he lets go her arm and tells her to walk forward so that he can see
her against that backdrop of blue sea and the very edge of the prom
and the cones of the canvas huts nosing upwards from the beach. He
stands back on the grass so that he can look at her, narrowing his
eyes which are clustered everywhere with wrinkles from the effort to
focus, turning his head to one side the way painters do and certain
species of seabirds, and the updraught of the wind from the beach
to the edge of the prom lifts her dress violently so that she limps
towards him, laughing. But he barks at her with a voice he might
use for servants and tells her to stand there and forget about the
wind and so she stands there, her dress billowing over her knees and
watches his smile, an old man's smile at a young woman, who has for
once seen a perfect pair of knees—

Technically, too, this group of prints is an immense improve-
ment. You've forgotten your reticence in the face of objects. I can
see it, that you focus with such a clarity on one that all the objects
around her fall into place. You do not see it, perhaps, but Father
Beausang's remarks on Poincaré have been proved correct since the
intractability of the world you looked at through your shutter seems
to have given way, as if a veil has been lifted. And where you caught
Luke clumsily, sixteen years ago, in a Moses basket and a woman's
hand comes awkwardly into the picture from the left-hand corner,
now you catch the woman unashamedly, face-on, and the world falls
into place behind her, just like, in fact, the landscape behind the cave

in Leonardo's 'Virgin of the Rocks'. How can Bray and its environs, the Dargle valley, the eucalypti around Killiney hill and the wildness of your back garden suddenly assume this neatness, this aptness, how can this solid world suddenly know its place—a place firmly behind the people that inhabit it—when for years it has edged quite brazenly and vulgarly into your vision, the horizon always at an angle, walls, trees and the ever-present seascape always at odds with and sometimes even crushing the faces you placed alongside them? I assume you didn't notice this change, and that the pleasure you always took in your photography was for once lost in the pleasure you took in the objects you photographed.

There are three photographs of the chair-lift. There is Rene with Luke in two and in the third Rene with your father. In the first Luke is sitting bolt upright in the yellow chair and staring without expression towards you, towards the camera. Rene is holding a black bag on her lap, looking towards the camera with a quiet smile. The yellow chair would have been swaying slightly, for the Bray that we can see behind them in the space between Luke and Rene is somewhat blurred and because of that even more like a miniature town, a miniature world. They are both staring at me now from the print as they must have stared at you, and Luke's face seems to express some resentment towards me, as father would to son, but perhaps I am only interpreting that as resentment in the light of what I know happened later. And Rene is looking at me with a smile which seems to contain whatever is between us two.

The chair is swaying in the next snap too and this time what is blurred is Rene herself, for her head is hanging over it and Luke is pulling at her elbow in mock horror. She is at the opposite end of the car this time, for Bray Head is behind them, fragments of what could be Wicklow, Wexford, dissolving into a blur, neither sea nor land. And in the third, the old man dominates, proud as he was on the promenade. He is pointing away from the sea towards the hinterland, the Sugarloaf and Lord Meath's estate. She is leaning past him to look and he must be describing the property he owned there and giving a gleeful account of the ways he managed to get rid of it.

Again there is nothing extraordinary in her face against the town of matchboxes with the railway station in the very centre and the line coming into it from Killiney and drawing away again towards Wicklow. Neither against the quite delicate line of the mountains on the other side of the chair-lift, going down this time, does she look extraordinary, Djouce, Tunduff and the Sugarloaf behind, its small peak of granite nibbling at the blue.

Which is not to deny the pleasure you took in those photographs. Whatever the object of your pleasure, your pleasurable eye is obvious. She fills them and the perspective with which you viewed her must be one of love. As if you have tried to embrace her, she leans through the prints, almost falling out of them. And the figures around her are blurred, as if the camera was jealous.

31

I MEDITATE ON HER in a way and invent her in parts as you must know by now, for the secret must be out. And if it is out, I'm not sure whether I've failed, and if it's not out, I'm not sure whether I've succeeded. Anyway, if James was jealous, and jealousy I imagine is a faded, parched colour, that precise tint that all his snaps have acquired over the years, mainly, let me say, through the accumulation of dust, he was jealous of every brick in the world he looked at, of every image because he couldn't possess it and jealousy next to love is the most loving of all emotions. He was jealous of the world because he couldn't love it as he needed to and he was also jealous of her. But his jealousy for her was of a more delicate kind and even now, in these prints, was wheeling round to the point it would eventually reach, where its bulk would become thin and eventually invisible. You can imagine then that I am also jealous, having her take the Bray train each weekend over that summer in which Father Beausang stopped his visits for good. The perspiration which the heat from the window would have induced in her, her light cotton dress, blue with perfectly round splashes of white all over and the coarse material in the seat from which every movement of hers caused dust to spring. It is a moving picture I have of her, since she holds a battered dictionary, English-Irish, turns pages and sighs continually as she reads for, as Lili tells me, she was never a great reader and the Irish lessons she gives to the Vance boy will be as bizarre and laughable as her own mastery of that language is. She is turning the pages anyway and constantly shifting from the page, to look at the procession of sea outside, sheared now and then by a thrust of beach or a stretch of heather when the tracks go inland. The insides of trains never hold for her the associations that the train viewed from just below the tracks does and so she loses her constant expectation of roses from the train windows the minute she enters. For not even the best of us can picture the outside from in and there is no way she could have seen, as they passed Killiney Head, the wheels shredding the lost strips of eucalyptus bark. But it would be unreasonable for the carriage in which she travelled and the polka-dot dress and the bristling chair not to retain the sense of those roses. And so I am jealous of every detail in any of those carriages in which she sat, all the more so since the Dublin-Bray train has been sheared of all its niceties over the years, the chairs now being movable and plastic and not even arranged in rows but fixed, backs to the wall, in a way that's more appropriate to a public bus. Bray has grown, you see. But the promenade's still there and the train that leads to it, and though it's more like a metal box than train carriages should be, it still has the bolt-marks in the floor where the seats that were more proper to it were fixed. I prefer to stand at the door with my hand on the window-sash and my cheek against the glass. That way I can see the procession of water outside, sheared by the beach, by occasional houses and stretches of green. And by the wonderfully squat governmental brick of the railway stations. Is there anything as sad as that red-brick, as the fawn, uneven granite of the platform and the tracks then, with the blue to one side? The tracks were given to private tender, but those stations must be governmental. The schoolgirls rise and leave at each and nobody gets on. And this empty carriage with its plastic chairs will become the object of someone else's envy in turn as they wonder how it was then. But my urge anyway is to possess the lost carriage in which she travelled that summer and the dress which caught her perspiration as it passed Glasthule, Killiney, Shankhill. Once past Killiney the land becomes less crowded and the tracks seem to fall gently with the land, towards the sea and towards Bray. The pages of the dictionary turning and turning, rustling even now over the plastic seats. Those lessons must have been just an excuse for the tall man who met her on hard times just after her mother's death. He felt the urge to help her and also the urge to possess. Lili thinks so, Father Beausang imagines so and I imagine so too. But then we are all faintly jealous. It is through jealousy that we draw near her and because of jealousy, perhaps, that we never reach her. I have no doubt that his first instinct was the generous one, that shambling, uncertain generosity of his that Lili remembers with distaste. The payment was fixed at ten shillings a lesson, an amount that for a man like him is never enough, since the generous urge is even more bottomless than the acquisitive one. And no doubt after the first one he increased it, slipped twice as much into the brown envelope that neither of them seemed to notice, that was left with her name on it on the table by the hatstand. That the lessons themselves were an embarrassment she never realised of course, and none of them would have dreamed of mentioning it to her. The boy suffered gladly the Saturday afternoon spent learning words from Abacus to Acclamation, since her idea was to progress through the dictionary alphabetically and she hadn't an inkling of grammar. And of course the beauty of that method was that there was never enough time, a lifetime wouldn't have sufficed, and by the end of the second Saturday they had only reached Artichoke. And so her visits became weekend ones, she would come on the Saturday morning and leave on the late train on Sunday, the extra lesson on Sunday afternoon being deemed absolutely necessary even to crack the sheen of that glorious mass of words. And of course after the third weekend, habit had set in and all four of them expected her and the current words would be repeated round the household like a litany. The old man even showed a surprising interest in Irish, the language he had hardly known existed. And habit brought its odd rituals too, the main among them being that the old man pestered her each Sunday to sit for him, and that Luke reserved for himself the right to wait for her at the station every Saturday morning and accompany her down Bray prom.

And because the last mile of the journey is over land that's falling gently the train seems to slide towards Bray where the last few schoolgirls get off. The sea disappears behind the backs of houses and then appears again. I get out of the metal carriage to where Luke used to wait on the granite platform and pass through the curved awning under which they both walked to the sun, the square and Bray.

⚹

LUKE TAKES HER elbow and leads her outside the station down a small road and past the bowling green. They turn right, through a narrow tunnel over which the same train runs farther down the coast. The curved avenue of light widens as they pass through and spills on to the beach where the light becomes fawn, blue and silver. Luke is tall now, almost as tall as his father, but with what characteristics? He neither paints nor photographs, as if the law of resistance between successive fathers and sons has come to rest in him. He has a disturbing restfulness of gesture that illuminates him in any drawing-room, never belonging to it, yet rooted to it. His father's unwillingness to open doors has given way in him to this stasis, never demanding to be more than where he is, yet disturbing whole companies with this seeming passivity. He stares from corners, fearful and self-possessed. An agoraphobic child, he has learnt to control this tendency by walking down each street with an extreme slowness, as if it were a room. And so he walks down this room that is a beach, holding her elbow for support, leading her towards the water, yet tightening his grip on her elbow as they draw near. That luminous child Lili has called him, and his eyes do stand out against the grey texture of his skin, metal-blue, like mirrors. This effeminate boy, grown tall in the way of some hothouse plants, could he have been different, I wonder, as James must have done. Could his hair have been thicker, his shoulders broader? James stares at him across the familiar gulf, all his words turn to questions, held in mid-air. Those planes of distance surround them, all angles, unbridgeable expanse.

But Luke is thin and has come to the largest expanse of all, the sea, and so holds her elbow even more tightly for support. Soon her elbow will be indistinguishable from his, his father's. There are the voices of the Scottish holiday-makers behind them and of the Jewish girls whom his grandfather loved to paint. A small paddle-boat that has gone too far out inches its way across the ribbon of blue. A man swings a leather bag beside them, calls at it to return.

32

SOME BRAY BUSINESSMAN had revitalised the lift. Will we ascend? asked Father Beausang and sprang up the metal steps with a vitality that amazed me. You are old, I began, but he was already in the yellow chair, patting the seat beside him. I was left to pay the man with the leather bag, who pulled the lever that sent us off, swaying.

'I lied to you,' he said, 'when I said I hadn't seen her. It was the house that made me melancholy and melancholy leads me to white lies. I had seen her, of course. How could I have lived in Bray and not seen her? I passed her on the prom and I see now that it must have been her first day here. But it was more a fiction than a lie and there's a kind of truth in fiction isn't there? I was hot on the prom, wearing that ridiculous black suit that always made me feel, in summer, like Descartes sweltering inside his stove. It helped him to think, he claimed. But my black suit and the sweat that ran from my collar down my shirt never helped me to think. I always walked quickly through the heat, racing to be inside once more. Though I'm sure it was her that seemed to bounce through the crowd of Scotsmen in open-necked shirts and even gesture towards me as if wanting me to stop. But of course I didn't stop, the last thing I wanted to do was stop. It had been Descartes, I remember, with James that day and

the cucumber sandwiches had upset my stomach and I had notes to
write on our discussions, all of this besides being hot, so of course
I couldn't stop. But if you were to ask me had I seen her, I couldn't
truthfully say no. But the verb to see conjures up more than mere
vision. I walked the Head too, you see, every weekend, Saturdays
and Sundays, and never a weekend passed but one or other of the
Vances would sway over me in the yellow chair, almost always with
her. I would hear the voices from below, the words carried off on the
wind of course, so I couldn't eavesdrop. If I walked nearer the cliff,
I could see them in profile. She never had much hair, I could make
out that, if it was her. Nothing like the great bush of hair I always
associate with beauty. All I could make out was that it was a woman
and James, Luke or the painter with her in the chair. And sometimes
all four. What attraction this chair had for them I couldn't make
out. I mean the seaside inhabitants are never the ones to use the
paddle-boats—'

火

WE HAD CLIMBED higher and the yellow chair was swaying like a
train going at high speed. A gust of wind carried off his words for an
instant and so I couldn't hear. Rather than stare at his mouth, opening and closing silently, I leant over the side and saw the great pylons
with their feet in the earth, the clumps of purple heather and the
small track along the cliffs, bordering the sea, along which he must
have walked. I looked up to the right of his shoulder and saw the
town flowing out from it, something like a neckscarf, and beyond it
the city. I turned and saw the thin finger of the Sugarloaf and beyond

it Djouce, the Three-Rock, Tunduff. The attraction of course must have been analagous to the attraction of trains. Of course none of them would have bothered to ride it but her, being a visitor, and if she associated trains with roses, what would this airborne carriage with its iron seats, its cogs and its cable clicking with dark grease mean to her? The flower that would have sprung from this would have been unimaginable. It was too high to have earth in the chair, its petals would have been silk and black, perhaps. An eminently human flower which springs from thought, the swaying chair, the wind cleansing the brow and the sensation of flight. James Vance looks at her and sees it sprouting from her mouth, her opened lips, saying something he can't hear, containing it like a pot. She sees it in Luke, in James, in the grandfather, sprouting through their stiff collars in place of their faces and its stem hidden, but threading its way, she knows, to the base of their spine. The old man's mane dips and waves. with it thorny, irascible but with his barely hidden delight oozing from him like perfume. And James Vance thinks he can capture this texture of flowers as he raises his camera once more and snaps. But in the print, when it emerges, the yellow chair on which her hand rests is nothing more than metal and she just a young woman, as my priest friend says, without much hair but with an extraordinary texture to what hair she has—

'And when I think of it, there is no one in the town that wouldn't have seen her. The word even reached my Superior that the agnostics—Protestants—no one was ever quite sure how to categorise poor James—in the Villas had a young lady staying with them. Governess, the more discreet gossipers called her. Fancy-woman, said the local wits. And the mothers of the sodality claimed the old man had got himself another model. And I suppose the truth is she was a little of all three. A fiction there, with more than half a truth.'

I lied. There is the unmistakable scent of flowers from those prints. Or is it the dust that gathered in the album? Dried flowers?

'Whatever was the truth, it had all the makings of a scandal. Only if she was Catholic, of course. There had been a fuss some years before. About a model who turned out to be Jewish . . .'

The yellow chair bumped to a halt and I was thrown forward into his lap. He held me for a moment by the shoulders and smiled. I could see the moisture gathering at the corner of each eye. He turned my face towards the turf and heather, now just six feet below us.

'See,' he said, 'we've come down. And I think those two small tickets of yours entitle us to a cup of tea . . .'

He gestured towards the metal stairs. I stood up and helped him to his feet and would have helped him down the stairs, but he insisted I go first. We clambered down then, one after the other, and walked across the heather to the Eagle's Nest and two cups of tea.

33

I s it on the close wet texture of the sand it happens, just after high tide, or between tides when the glare is an aching yellow and the sand is hot under their bare feet? If it's Luke, he's with her in the early morning. Instead of lessons under the bay window they have walked out here; James has spent the night in Dublin, and the old man is still sleeping in his sick-bed. Luke stands in the water in his shoes. She calls him back, Luke, Luke, he is her charge after all. He walks back across the ridges, all the miniature pools, to where the sand is dry again and clings like fawn paper to his shoes. He leads her by the hand to beneath the promenade wall. The sun is hottest there, it catches the glare, sand and stone, and there is a lip to hide whoever's below from the strollers above. The sun seems moderately low over the seascape, it is morning as yet, the vapour hasn't gathered to a haze, the paddle-boats are beached, awaiting their owner's leather bag. Each line is as sharp as it could be. But lying down, the sun seems high and so lying down they make it suddenly mid-afternoon, the glare pulses in an almost clear blue and the mackerel clouds disperse. The tide from a broad board becomes a flat ribbon, the sands become hillocks of fawn, all perspectives reversed. Luke covers his body in a down of blonde sand.

火

AND FOR JAMES perhaps the canvas hut. Mid-afternoon, when the boatman's calling the paddle-boats to shore seems to fade into the haze. He is old, his face is as creased as his leather, his hands are hard and coin-coloured. The boats circle to his cries. James pushes aside the flapping door and walks into the world of canvas, conical, its light filtering through the blue and yellow in alternate stripes. Rene stands in the lit cone and his mind, as tendentious as ever, registers the colours, blue and yellow, echoes of the colours outside. James makes love with words, perhaps, he uses the unique syllable with tongue, lips and teeth, he manages her first name only with difficulty, Miss O'Shaughnessy he seems happier with since he pays her, after all, to teach Luke. But what coinage could allow him to approach her, none but her own, which could hardly be named as she gives it to father or son or father and son. James's voice is muffled by the canvas there and the sand beneath his feet. The cries from the beach outside are almost louder than his, but his cries are words. The skin across her back is ridged by the imprint of her shoulder blades. There are canvas deckchairs, folded in a heap. Somewhere above him a train rumbles.

火

BUT THE HEATHER could have held all three of them. We made our way through it, mounds of it. Once again he showed himself younger than his years. I stumbled now and then but he trod on.

'And what are all scandals about but love? Love, sacred and profane, carried in words, all of them echoes of that greatest scandal of them all when the word was made flesh and the scandal was the word and the word was love. She visited them for the best part of the year until the fit-ups took her on that provincial tour. The old man died soon after and the Scots returned for their summer weekends. I walked the promenade, I sat in my rooms. I turned my mathematical inquiries to that exquisite system of triadic ambiguity that is Marian theology.'

He strode on, his boots raising clouds of dust, or was it pollen?

34

DESPITE LUKE'S FEAR of open spaces he must have ventured out that summer to a garden fête, a large open field where he seems restless even in the photograph, surrounded by upturned temporary tables and crumpled cloths. There are Jesuits in the background and among them a female figure which could be Rene. He seems like a large thin bull there, who would make of the field a pattern on a living-room wall, if he could. His hair is thin and lank so that the bristling quiff, so evident above his forehead years ago, is all but hidden. He seems to be leaning towards the camera, imploring it to release him, perhaps so that he can get back to the security of those massed Jesuits. There is accusation in his eyes. He must have been held there for an inordinate length of time so that his father could get the focus right. The space of this field in which his father has placed him appals him, but no more than the spaces of the world into which his father has thrown him. And he stands, apparently tottering forward for what seems an age before the shutter clicks, and then turns and walks stiffly, as rapidly as he can without running, towards the black mass of the Jesuits and the white tables.

He meets their crowded backs with relief, their serge shoulders, shiny rather than black from rubbing against one another. The sandwiches on the long tables have gone soft in the heat but the Jesuits keep eating them and the maids keep running for more. These maids are squat and have freckled faces and wear aprons identical in shape if not in design. They approach the Fathers with slightly bowed heads, transport the blue and white plates with banana sandwiches, but once out of earshot they clasp each others' hands, they giggle, running towards the refectory for more. The Fathers stand in groups, scattered round the white tables, round the mothers of the schoolboys. They stare at this agoraphobic boy, seeing in him perhaps a lost pupil and possibility. But he just stands there clutching the white tablecloth, inhaling the odour of Jesuit serge, looking for the small circle of massed priests among whom he hopes is Rene.

James Vance brings tripod and box down past the longest of the tables and is approached by a lay brother who fifteen years ago took minor Abbey parts. I tend the garden now, this brother tells him, I dig trenches and grow vegetables for the community meals. Do you remember that snap you took of *The Workhouse Ward* where I could be seen in the background talking to the Peeler? The priesthood is not for everyone, this lay brother tells him, and not for such as me who grew up in that profane trade.

The Superior is tall and rigid and one half of his crown is bald. Perhaps the only one of the Fathers who hasn't eaten sandwiches, he walks among the tables towards James, holds him gently by the elbow. Hopkins, he tells him, *was* a poet. Swinburne, for whom I've heard you profess such a liking, has been responsible for the most blasphemous line in the last two thousand years. He quotes softly as if his lips are trying to separate themselves from the words.

Thou hast conquered, O pale Galilean;
the world has grown grey from thy breath.

The Superior's crown gleams like a mirror with perspiration. His hand is firm and irritating. We must come to some arrangement, he lowers his voice, about all school photographs . . .

A young athlete from the Sixth Form walks between the tables and the knots of priests. He is still dressed for running and perspiration and effort have stiffened his hair into a mass of blond curls. He acknowledges none of the Fathers' nods, and yet the Fathers seem not to mind. Vigour, they seem to say, and youth obey their own laws. A glow of vapour and distilled effort surrounds him. A yearly figure, the Superior whispers, for portraits of all the forms . . .

Luke walks between two maids, carrying empty plates. Take me to the house, he asks them. They walk beyond the tables, clasping their hands behind his back. One is taller than him, the other smaller. Do you all wear the same sized apron? he asks, noticing how the small one is wrapped in hers, the tall one choked by hers. No, says the tall maid, laughing, there's two sizes. Too big and too small. She has a brace and her consonants click. They cross the large field, beyond the tables. Their clasped hands separate and fall around his waist.

火

THE SUN CURVES gradually downwards and as the day grows cooler the Fathers disperse, Jesuit by Jesuit, from their small groups. The Sixth Form athlete walks towards the field exit arm in arm with a middle-aged, elegant lady. His mother, the lay brother whispers, shaking his head, is a saint. Our persuasions are different, the Superior muses. He tries to disguise his curiosity. The young woman who came with you, she's not a local girl?

Luke finds her in the kitchen, sitting at a wooden table, surrounded by the maids. Each maid is plucking her apron, laughing coarsely. Rene's smile seems to include each one of them. We seen you on the train, says the maid with the braces, you getting off it and us getting on—

35

A YOUNG WAITRESS BROUGHT us the tea. She walked between the small patio and the Eagle's Nest, bringing first the cups, then the tea and then the sugar and milk. It was a wooden building with a corrugated iron roof which sang whenever it rained. Luckily enough the sun had again come out so we sat outside. The whole arrangement was quite a suntrap since the Head loomed over the Eagle's Nest, shielding it from the prevailing winds, and the Eagle's Nest loomed over the patio. I asked the serving-girl had they had many trippers and she said no, that we were the first yet. Could you drink outside like this, I asked her, in the old days? I don't remember, she answered. She seemed annoyed by the question and I couldn't understand why until I realised she couldn't have been born then. Is this your first job then? I continued when she came with the milk. What's it to you? she muttered, her young eyes narrowing.

We plucked the sprigs of heather from our trousers while she poured the tea. Between the last pylon of the lift and the Eagle's Nest there was nothing but heather, two or three feet deep. We both agreed that there must have been a track there once and that a new one would appear soon when the lift caught on again.

But we sat in silence once the girl had poured the tea, he hardly touching his cup, sitting with his face to the bay and his eyes half-closed. I wondered was he tired or was our silence caused by our sudden intimacy some moments back, just when the lift stopped? Or perhaps by the young girl's annoyance? I put my face close to his but only the whites of his eyes showed through his half-opened lids; they didn't register the blue bay before them. Perhaps old priests are like old horses, I thought, they sleep at odd moments only, in postures of waking. So I put his saucer on top of his cup to keep it warm and went ahead and drank my own tea. It was scalding, though a little weak.

Time passed and clouds flitted over the heather, like heather themselves. Father Beausang stayed asleep. I sensed someone looking at me then and turned to see the serving-girl in the wooden doorway with a camera raised to her face. The camera clicked as I turned and she ran into the interior, clutching it to her breast. I rose from my seat quietly so as not to waken him and walked towards the door, and inside.

I stood just inside the doorway looking across the wooden floor and the round tables to where she sat, behind the counter. Move over, she said, you're blocking the light. I walked forward and the light flooded in behind me, which seemed to satisfy her since her air of annoyance faded and she focused on the camera in her hand with a kind of innocent concentration. Is this your first job then? I asked again, but she silenced me with a Shhh! and placed the camera on the counter where I could see it. It was an instant one I saw, streamlined and plastic with an aperture from which the print would slide out. We both watched the print slide out then and fall on to the wooden counter, as if it had a will of its own. It was a wonderful grey colour which gradually changed as if smoke was drifting across it and the gaunt shape of the pylon loomed out of the smoke and the broken shape of the coastline and the softer shapes of two figures at a table. For a terrible moment I feared that the pylon would be as it was in its heyday and the heather would be worn to a track by countless feet and the figures at the table would be those of Luke and Rene. But no, I saw my own surprised face and Father Beausang with his head towards the bay and the bay itself coloured in a glorious blue, more heightened, if anything, than the blue outside.

I ordered two more teas. Outside Father Beausang was still asleep. I would have liked to ask her who had revitalised the lift when she came up with the teas. But she was still wearing her air of youthful annoyance so I asked her instead why she took the picture. Because you, she answered, are my first customers. She gathered up the old cups and set down two new ones with a fresh pot of tea. Father Beausang woke with the disturbance. He turned his head away from the water, towards me. It's getting cooler, he said, and it was.

His eyes were fully open and looking towards the yellow chairs. They only moved, I surmised, when there was a passenger.

火

'So I HAVE seen her. The whole promenade must have seen her, in one way or another. Certainly my superior, a parish priest named Cartan had heard and seen enough of her to be worried. If she were Catholic and modelled each weekend for a Protestant painter, you see, something would have to be done. I had to inquire then, discreetly, into her background. And discretion suited me especially since, as you know, I couldn't visit the house any longer. It was not only a point of delicacy with me, it was my recognition that something had ended. My function in that house had been replaced by hers. Or to put it another way, the cup that I had half-filled, flowed right over with her. If I met James on the promenade or behind a bathing shelter we would continue our discussions for the length of a stroll, but meeting like that was never satisfactory. The room within bay windows was missing, you see, and the figure of Luke with his tray of sandwiches and tea, which incidentally—'

He drained his cup

'—was far, far better than this. And you can't talk mathematics walking down a promenade, surrounded by Scots. I wasn't jealous or resentful of her but I was intensely curious. I felt an odd affinity with her too. She was to take up my guardianship, after all, and I could sense from James on the promenade this air of blossoming after all those years. No matter how far our discussions had ranged, you see, their original purpose had never been quite forgotten. He was still "talking instruction", I was still waiting for the staff to blossom. And there he was, blossoming after all those years.'

火

THE SMELL OF dried flowers that comes from your prints, after, as he says, all those years. How can the photographer himself blossom? He was rarely on the prom, a little like Luke in his preference for indoors. Summer smells too aren't often redolent of flowers. From where we sat I could smell the prom below us, the burnt metal of the amusement parlours and the wet sand in particular. But what the curate saw must have been like James Vance blossoming. He is forty-seven and it's the summer of nineteen thirty-three. Your angular walk along the prom and the hesitant stoop that Lili described in you. Pliant now, and perhaps that *is* the word for it. Two miles away is the hill with eucalypti, still divesting themselves of their stripes of bark. And they don't blossom either, they drop off cones, nowhere near as elegant as their stripes of bark. You could only photograph others in flower and never flower yourself.

火

'I WOULD BE lying if I said I wasn't faintly jealous. But then jealousy is the most loving of all emotions.'

He turned to me and smiled.

'Next to love, that is. But while one can be jealous of what one doesn't know, one can't really love whom one doesn't know. So my most overriding emotion was—'

He smiled again.

'—what I would say is yours—curiosity. And curiosity about her, happily enough, had become part of my pastoral duty. So I set about finding out about her.'

火

THE GIRL HAD brought more tea. She replaced the pot this time, but not the cups. Are these the original tables, I wanted to ask her, of the original Eagle's Nest? But she still wore that look of youthful annoyance so I desisted. A chill was coming in now, from the sea. Father Beausang poured for both of us. Those tickets were good value, he said, with the emphasis on the 'were'. I realised then that he had not realised he'd been asleep. 'The one pastoral duty I've ever enjoyed. And one of the many I've failed at. I found out a lot. I went to Dublin, interviewed a young aspiring actress called—'

'Lili,' I said.

'Yes, Lili. I found out that our Rene was Catholic. I found out that if the old man painted her it was at odd moments and never unclothed. When I found out who her father was my pastoral duty stopped, since the children of the blessed are above suspicion, so to speak. But of the whole story I could only get a glimpse. Months later I heard the real fact—that she was pregnant—'

火

THE SUN HAD touched the Head and the light was coming down in movable fingers of infinite length, since they caressed the bay as much as they caressed us. We sat watching the shifting glory. I glanced behind me and saw the serving-girl, standing behind us. She was as awed as we were, with no camera. All three of us watched, Father Beausang with his face towards the bay. I felt the time had come. Your boss, I whispered to her. Who is he? And sure enough she smiled, her face towards the bay, and whispered a name.

SIX

THE PROVINCES, 1934

36

A ND SO SHE was pregnant and waiting in Dublin to tour the country. There would be three of them soon, father, son and Rene, awaiting the arrival of the child, the father of whom no one has been able, or willing to name. And time becomes stilled for them while she grows, yet all they discover is one of its more secret rhythms. They are mastered by a unit as basic as a day, a month, a year, but of which they are only now made conscious. It must have seemed marvellously arbitrary to them, nine months, two hundred and seventy days. They think of the pregnancies of elephants and whales, butterflies and moths and feel that in an odd way they have annihilated time. They fall instead into an element of the same fluidity and texture as that expanse of water they have seen for years beyond Bray Head, that the yellow chairs have bobbed over, that Rene has watched from Trimelston Road, that other sea in which the world will immerse itself, basking like a glistening dolphin. And Rene of course holds the secret of that time. She expands on the grace of her first three photos, moves to a point for which perspectives are useless.

大

BUT BEFORE THERE were three of them, there would be two. There would be Luke and Rene, moving in a narrowing circle, changing town and parish hall every second or third night. For a while she takes the boys' parts, but after the first three weeks when her condition becomes obvious, an improbable boy, MacAllister, with infinite grace and tact, promotes her to female parts proper and even gives her a rise. So now she can wear dresses with bodices in place of the adolescent's doublet and hose. The female wardrobe of costumes is limited to four, which must serve for all parts from Kathleen to Cleopatra. And all sense of period is totally ignored, be it Roman, Celtic, Elizabethan or Edwardian. The past is simply the past, counterpoised with the present. And for the present there is no wardrobe whatsoever, the cast swap their working clothes as the parts demand. Sad, MacAllister would whisper with his inimitable smile. But these are the provinces, dears. And these four past costumes are of four distinct types as if woman herself, whom they feigned to represent, can be categorised in four. There is Queenly Beauty, Aged Refinement, Nurse/Nun/Midwife, and Youthful Innocence. Rene, through her tour, uses versions of all four, changing character and lines as her figure dictates. Lucky, as MacAllister whispers, these are the provinces.

火

THERE WILL BE no photographs, since James doesn't reach them until near the end, and Luke's flight destroys his faith forever in the perceivable object. And is that significant as well, I wonder, as he loses his urge at last to grasp at years, to stick his moments into albums and annotate each one. Does he too feel the annihilation of time, staring from the green felt table out of the bay window, picturing both loved ones just through disappointment and desire? Nothing will revive his faith in photographs and when his faith itself revives, it will be with a strength that needs no photographs. His camera dies, and there is only the spoken word to replace it, and memory, and imagination. And all three are frighteningly elastic, handing us as a gift that freedom that annihilates more than time, the contours of our subjects themselves.

⚐

So Luke braves the Bray train alone. He walks behind the hotels, clinging to the walls of the terraced houses, treading like water the spaces of the wide streets, past the Turkish baths and the bowling green and into the station itself. I descended the Head with Father Beausang and back down the long promenade to where the station made a wooden roof above the tracks, curved, to enclose the sea in its frame. As Luke waits the rain comes and each pointed eave contains its drop. When our train came I helped Father Beausang up the step, through the door and into the carriage of plastic seats. We moved out of Bray then and towards Shankhill, through the houses, through the green to where blue expanse was on our right and the eucalyptus slopes were on our left. I thought of Luke on the wooden seat with his neck against the shoulder of felt. The rain comes and hammers the blue into the colour of tin. The scene moves past his moving window, a succession of granite platforms leading to the largest one of all, and there he rises and walks slowly to the door and through the clouds of reassuring steam into that corridor of glass. The steam

billows and fades as the train pulls towards Amiens Street and Luke
negotiates the platform and the slight incline of Westland Row down
to the backstage of the Ancient Concert Rooms in Rutland Street.

37

FATHER BEAUSANG SLEPT through Westland Row despite my efforts to wake him. So we got off at Amiens Street, stood together on the moving stairs and had to walk towards Lili's modest residence along the canal. The giant pots on O'Connell Bridge seemed burdened with their flowers, hanging limp in the heat like the flags that hung from each new building. He refused my offer of a taxi.

火

IMAGINE JAMES'S CAMERA swinging forlorn from the hatstand. It seems out of place there, squat, so contained in its leather case. All the coats that have hung there for years, their folds seem to stiffen as they hang, enclosing in a kind of stillness the fluted trunk of the stand. But the camera swings when he places it there, to and fro, glancing off the surface with each return. So he listens to the stand rocking faintly and looks at the unfinished mural his father left, the Connemara landscape forming a window, a gateway into this odd expanse of hills that his father imagined to be Greece; the woman's face pinioned between both as if he could never decide quite what background she needed. He can see now that it isn't quite her, the neck is too Grecian, the cheekbones are too flushed and Irish, she has been only caught in that fringe of blonde. James leaves the hall and goes into the living-room and the camera still swings from the hatstand. He pulls out the drawer in the cabinet and takes out a sheaf of papers, deeds of inheritance, mortgages, old litigations, the whole penumbra of unfinished business left untouched now for three generations. He leafs through signatures of gentlemen and Papists, Bray burghers, certificates of birth, marriage and death until he comes to a small compact pile of invoices and inventories of stock all filled in in the fine nib and hand of a long-forgotten clerkship. The stock of the forgotten pottery he finds was numbered at seventeen hundred units, 'unit' being specified as a set complete with cups, saucers, side plates and serving bowls. Their value he finds assessed in pounds, in single numbers, the total stock having been rendered almost worthless by the influx of machine-made delft from the English midlands. The whorls and curlicues of the unknown clerk's hand remind him of the fine blue lines on the delft itself, that solid grace and attention to detail that seem to him to have walked across water to here from an unknown country. He should take the train now and get off at Killiney and stand on the moulting hill again among the stripes of eucalyptus, inhaling again that scent of resin and tomcats, the wet dust of the bay. But he doesn't, it's not yet time for him to take the train. He goes upstairs and urinates in the bowl, surrounded by the odour of fathers, of the slow drip across the years, of inheritance, colouring and temper, from father to son and father to son.

⚘

WE WALKED FROM O'Connell Bridge to College Green and Clarendon Street. As we passed the brash, coloured pietà in the courtyard of the church, I stopped him and pointed at her curved plaster mouth. If the Father, I asked him, fathered His own Son and yet the Son was the Father, does that mean the Son fathered Himself? Something like annoyance crossed his face, and then a hint of a smile. I apologised for my lack of acquaintance with what I remembered he had called that exquisite system of triadic ambiguity, and tried to rephrase it. In other words, I asked, if the Son fathered Himself, did He by that very act create His own Father? He smiled fully then and pulled me on. You are leaving out, he whispered, the third corner of that exquisite triangle: the Holy Spirit.

༝

LUKE FINDS THE front-of-house doors barred and makes his way along the side. From somewhere he can hear brass music. He walks with his hand against the russet brick that leads him to the stage entrance. The door is open and he hears voices coming from the inside gloom. He gets the odour then and I can shiver at the precise feel of that rust crumbling dryly at the touch of her fingers and the roses as she leant close and smelt them as their bowls blew soundlessly over the leather. But it is the dust Luke smells, of an unused stage. He runs his hand along the metal bar, walking inside.

༝

WE REACHED LILI'S house and shook hands and I watched him walk across the bridge, over the grey ribbon of canal. He seemed fatigued all of a sudden. I had promised to call him when all the questions were finished, when I came back from Clare, but looking at his slow, dark walk I realised how little promises mean to the old. He didn't turn or wave, so I rang the bell and listened for Lili's difficulty in coming down the stairs.

38

'CAN YOU IMAGINE,' said Lili, quite unnecessarily, rocking softly once more in her cane chair, 'the impact of that extraordinary boy on that group of Thespians? You know what Rene meant to them, but can you imagine how the effeminate hams fawned over him, delighted in him, loved him even? The boy was their dream, they would have had him as Ophelia in a white dress strung with real watercress and lilies. But then he'd never, no matter what the inducement, go beyond carrying sets. Besides which he would have been a terrible actor. He hung around walls even more than his father did, which might be why it suited him. He'd stand behind flats, walls within walls, and watch the open stage from there. But can you imagine that gaggle of cynical, poverty-stricken actors, dedicated to nothing but the next night, willing to sell their grandmothers for the dual ends of simple survival and the practice of what they called their "art"—can you imagine them roused to all the possibilities of innocence by a love affair between their A.S.M. and their second lady? It was a conspiracy, you see, enacted on the Free State, on that society we played to. We moved through those towns, the names of which I can hardly remember, like early Christians carrying the message. But the message was sent out in an elaborate code. After the first few shows it came out that she was pregnant. Now that's a message we couldn't have spelt out. But can you imagine the pleasure in conveying it while disguising it? The happy falsity, the artifice? We did botched-up versions of the comedies, *Measure for Measure*, *As You Like It*, we did all the old staples, *The Colleen Bawn*, *The Workhouse Ward*, *The Rising of the Moon*, *The Countess Cathleen*. But no matter what story each of them told, the same story always told itself through them. Which was love, I suppose. And I can never think of that word outside a story.'

火

LUKE, YOU SEE, has found his home. The man with the flowing mane of hair and the velvet jacket and the cigarette forever in its holder who meets him just inside the stage door reminds him of his grand-father. He withdraws his hand quickly on the handshake and orders him briskly to come inside. And Luke walks into the gloom and feels instantly, unmistakably, in the home of his emotions verified. That cluttered world of dust, spiralling from the bare yellow light bulb, all his movements constricted by the canvas flats. He finds truth in the falsity he finds there. The number of flats is limited, he notices, a few bare, timeless scenes having to serve any number of purposes. There is a living-room wall with an ornate window, and through the window a vista of beach and sea. This serves, he is told, for worlds as varied as the drawing-rooms of Sheridan to, at a push (and it is a push, MacAllister smiles), the court of the Duke of Mantua. There is a garden of course, vague enough to belong to any period, defined only by a stretch of green, a border of flowers and an arch of trel-lis tumbling with roses. And there is a cluster of white Doric pillars against a background of blue which must be by turn ecclesiastical, courtly, or plain Athenian.

A man in a check jacket whose name must be Brogan emerges from the gloom and Luke watches him stabilise flats, sees how to intimate an infinity of spaces from a handful of canvas rectangles and some square yards of stage. The dust is drifting from the footlights to the hanging lights and Luke stands in the cones of dust and sees Brogan carry that deeply satisfying vista of beach and sea and drawing-room window from stage left to stage right.

⚘

'It was simply a tour, like any other. I remember the trains, towns flitting past the windows. We played all the parish halls and stayed one night in each—Clones, Birr, Ballina—what do I know about names? All I know was MacAllister's grand plan which hadn't changed for donkeys' years and which was to push through the midlands, do all the seaside towns in summer and do September in Lisdoon. But don't ask me for details. I remember successions of small hills. Small crowds. Until we came to Knock. Then we all noticed.'

39

I AM LOST IN the midlands but I found Knock to be a small
stretch of houses, miles from the main line, awaiting the cente-
nary of an apparition of the Virgin there in 1879. I walked through
it at night and found it lit by those flashing coloured bulbs that more
humble townlands reserve for the apparition of a fun fair. Wooden
stalls formed a wedge down the centre, a positive danger to those
motorists who sped through it towards Mayo. She was there in every
conceivable pose, rows of her upon the stalls, lit now by bulbs from
the inside, now by luminous paint, in metal, in plastic and all kinds of
alloy. They ranged from the very cheap to the moderately expensive,
and I chose one of the expensive ones. She was blue and glowed from
the inside and was standing on a pedestal. Walking through the stalls
I found it easy to convince myself that each one celebrated quite a
different visitation—the one of Rene, Luke and Emerald Theatrical
Productions Ltd, all of whom stopped, I surmised, at the small
wooden hall wedged behind the giant grey church which stood some
yards from where the row of stalls ended. It would be appropriate, I
thought, that every stall and every statue sold remembered an event
that the visitors and the stall owners had quite forgotten. I knew
that the urge to visit shrines is deeper and more crass than memory.
And there was an empty touring bus by the church and it pleased me

to think of those busloads celebrating an event of which they knew absolutely nothing, though it pained me to think that the trains had stopped and that somewhere outside the town was a disused pale granite station, beside a canal perhaps. All this though my statue didn't resemble her at all. And sure enough, when I had reached the end of the coloured lights and the street had become a country road, I came upon parallel ruts in the road through which tracks must have run. And I looked through the hedge and saw the tracks running eastwards, rusted of course, with the small pale granite station dripping under trees and beside it the canal.

火

LUKE CARRIES THE flat with the Grecian pillars from the train on to the platform and through the dripping trees. His cheek touches the canvas. And the feel of the paint reassures him as he walks through the pines with their eternal drip. He walks from sleeper to sleeper until he reaches the road and then carries his pillars down into the church, the small wooden hall. I see him walking back then through the pines to where they all stand on the fawn platform, jaded, laughing gently. Brogan hands him flat after flat from the train, which is gently steaming. The others strut on the platform, watching the moon through the pines.

火

THERE'S A NOTICE on the lamp post which flaps, a little like a flag. Rene is to play Rosalind. Those dusty halls have bare wooden stages and the chairs are sometimes cinema chairs, joined with one long iron band against each felt back. When I ran my finger along the felt chair-backs small puffs of dust rose endlessly. The dust is a problem. It rises from the wooden stage, catches all the light. The stage itself echoes with each footstep and so Rene walks slowly on it, each movement plumbed with stillness. Most of the bulbs are burned out and so the stage is lit in pools with vacuums in between. MacAllister paces the back rows conceiving his version of the miracle through which the Duke will be exiled to a manifest Forest of Arden and the wrestling match will be a wrestling match. He is smoking and squinting and striking the felt seat impatiently when Rene walks into the inadequate lights and begins her lines. He sees her walking from the gloom to the light and notices the odd retraction of her movement. Then he sees her blonde hair and flushed cheeks in the moving eddies of dust under the lights and the dust seems to carve out a space for her, anticipating each movement, leaving a faint glow behind. MacAllister, sitting in the dark among the felt seats, realises with a sudden shock that it is the glow of her pregnancy. The lights above grip her, form a cone around her of gently wheeling dust as if they could lift her upwards but she stays on the bare boards, full and three-dimensional against the sagging curtains and the painted flats. There is a heightened flush to each of her words and every gesture she makes is somehow round, flows and yet has the glow and presence of someone standing still.

火

'THE CENTRE OF the stage was wherever she was, just that, your eyes were drawn towards her and when she moved all the lines were made redundant. Now she wasn't an actress in the normal sense of the word, in any sense even. She had inherited all her mother's faults, but where Una had the unhappy knack of turning every part into a public speech, Rene had the gift of turning each into simply herself. She had come to it by accident and stayed with it by accident. And now this self of a sudden spilled and flowed, is the only word for it, out further than the stage and those perpetually faulty lights. A happy occurrence, you might think. But what terrified us was that every line and move of hers had nothing to do with the story in question. She was telling a different, quite simple story. Every part of her said simply: I am pregnant.

'Of course we all thought of the obvious: headlines in the provincial papers, sermons from the pulpit and theatrical riots. So when the hall was half-full as usual and there was the usual half-bored, half-ritual air of a fairground or a charity concert, we were all lit by a kind of terror backstage. What she seemed to reveal every time she moved into the footlights we were determined to conceal. And what emerged, happily, was nothing to do with our fears. From the word go that stage was heightened. The facts we knew meant nothing to the two hundred odd subscribers down there. But what the facts led to did. They didn't see her pregnant, they saw her simply resplendent. And they saw every other performance stretched to a pitch to conceal the secret. Since they couldn't glean the secret, all they could glean was the pitch, the richness. What they couldn't read of the real story made the apparent story all the more enthralling. And so when the curtain went down, if our sigh of relief was audible, the applause from the wooden hall was more than adequate to drown it.'

40

I PUT THE STATUE on the mantle and felt the warmth coming from it. I asked Lili what the next town was. She demurred. I saw the pines again, dark green against the moon, dripping on to the pale granite platform, the tracks wet and silver, running towards another town.

火

'SAY IT WAS Boyle. And if it was Boyle I've no picture of it anyway. Except maybe for a market. Yes, say there was a market and a main street with a chemist's shop and the train station was red-bricked, if you say so. But I can see a school hall, yes a hall that was used as a church once, the real church burnt down in the Troubles. Or was it just the high windows darkened with brown paper that reminded me of churches?'

火

THEY COME TO Boyle, maybe, where the hands of the dealers slap the bullocks' thighs and are spat on and shaken. There is Luke and the company walking through a square with streets running from all four corners. They get dispersed of course in the mêlée of cattle, so many packed between the shop fronts that there can be no sense of an open passage. They lean to each other over the rumps of cattle and shout, unsure of which corner of the square to go towards. The ground is churned into ankle-deep mud and MacAllister is pretending impatience, his blue suit smudged by the flicking bullocks' tails and his grey hair blowing. But they are all laughing, stretching over hides and laughing, touching hands when they can and falling back when the motion of a bullock shifts them, laughing in the mud. This way, boy, MacAllister whispers to Luke, to whom the pressure of the hide is even healthier than the shoulders of priests. Luke follows him, carrying his flats towards the rectangular front of the Roscommon Arms Hotel.

火

'It would have been unthinkable, any other year, that he'd change his plans. But now it was unthinkable that he wouldn't.'

火

In the lounge of that hotel which would have had a twelve-pound salmon, dried ochre scales gleaming with resin, its mouth permanently open behind the glass, he has his maps open and Luke is somewhere near as tall as him and with the same lank hair, and between them there is even a slight familiar air. If Boyle takes two days, Mountcharles will have to be skipped, but then there is Ballina, which might even take three. And the pattern of towns and halls, memories of good nights and bad, dates on which they'll be full and empty and the logic with which he's bound them together over years slowly falls asunder and he can see, just barely, the dim outlines of the pattern that's to replace them. They must reach the sea, he knows, by mid-July and trace a thread of towns down the coast towards Clare. He plans in advance for this new element and then, looking towards Luke, who is gazing at the open salmon's mouth in the glass case, he senses that no matter how he plans, a pattern of which he can gauge perhaps nothing will establish itself. And that night in the hall, pacing, as Lili says, behind the end seats he hears Rene's lines, Well, I will forget the condition of my estate to rejoice in yours, and it strikes him that no matter how he times it, days, nights, weeks and months, there is a logic there that will draw them all from town to town at its own pace, a pace he knows nothing about and can only wait to discover. She is standing in the dark pool between the foot-lights and yet can be seen clearly with that roundness of gesture that nobody could photograph. Luke, standing behind his canvas trees, can see her clearly, the whole hall can see her, against all the laws of theatrical lighting and effect.

‹

'AND IT COULD well have been Boyle because now that I think of it, the first of the write-ups we got was in the *Roscommon Herald*. Now that is a fact, though please don't expect a yellowing cut-out, I never was one for keeping things. But I remember that one because it was the first of the write-ups, and write-ups for those summer tours of ours were more or less unheard of. Part-time journalists for those

provincial papers used to writing up silage, sprout seasons and the
county hunt began to shove small columns in the pages they normally reserved for litigations, commenting on the fact that instead of
one night we stayed for three, that the audiences spilled outside the
stage doors, things like that. Captions like "Resplendent Rosalind",
"MacAllister Breaks Through", that kind of thing. Later, Dublin
critics came to write us up but that was when Rene was bigger and
we had touched the edge of Clare. The first was in the *Roscommon
Herald* and said that Rene's Rosalind would make Shakespeare en-
joyable even to those whose reading had never gone beyond a train
timetable.'

41

THEY PUSH TOWARDS the sea in half-circles. The texture of
the platforms changes as they circle nearer of course, and the
neat flower beds of the midlands stations give way to blackthorns,
all bending eastwards with the prevailing winds. Stations in the small
resorts on the western seaboard, so poignant to imagine, don't, re-
grettably, exist. To get to Strand Hill, for instance, which Lili mentions as their first holiday venue, you have to get off near Ballisodare
and the grey blocks there, I imagine, must be weeping with the salt
and water in the winds and though there would be alder as well as
blackthorn and the blackthorns themselves would be relatively upright there must have been a hint, perhaps just in the emptiness of the
station itself and the tracks running through the scrublands, waiting
for trains, of the texture of coast itself. Luke holds his flat against the
wind and is pulled by it down to where the platform ends, almost on
to the tracks themselves. So he has to point his canvas drawing-room
straight at the wind to walk forward at all.

He hugs it with him to the two hired cars that are waiting. The
drivers both wear caps and the company are standing around the
doors, hugging their clothes against the wind. The wind beyond the
granite walls pulls the flat again and Luke flies for a minute, the drawing-room in the air above him. He feels stretched like a bird, in one

clean line, and bounces in a series of airborne steps to the company, the capped drivers and the cars.

☼

THESE BLACK FORDS took over after the farthest stations ended. It is the first road Luke has driven with them, from Ballisodare to the coast, and the fabric of the interior seems to come apart before his eyes, through the car window, as if the strands which held the pines and the blackthorn and the broken hills are being pulled out leaving simply fields, smooth and rolling towards the largest sea. The drivers would have known the company over a succession of years, both of them squinting through the rearview mirror, their curiosity hidden by their caps. They recognise old faces and examine new ones and have to swerve continually since their obsession with their rearview mirrors threatens to leave them in the ditch. And they come to the line of the sea then that is broken by what seems to be, just where it meets the sand, this continual surge of white, the effect of the wind on that body of water that seems to Luke to form one long wave that he imagines must surge north and south, spanning the coastline, from this small patch of cement and sand where the cars finally pull to a halt.

☼

'AND THE ONLY reason I remember Strand Hill is because of the two drivers who were brothers who took us from the train to the hotel. They seemed to wear the same cap and to be always holding it with the same hand against the wind. You see, there was always wind there, it must have been on a kind of headland, because there was more wind there than on any of those western towns that I remember, but then maybe I only remember the wind because of the two brothers and their caps. There was more wind than rain but the wind was the kind that even on the finest days seemed to saturate the air with spray. And this could be quite a relief on a hot day and on a wet day you blamed the rain anyway, not the poor innocent sea, but the effect it did have was to make the walls of all the buildings damp. Weeping granite, somebody called it, which quite catches the reality—these grey hotel fronts with large patches of damp facing the sea. And the patches of damp were, if you will allow me the simile, a little like the smears a child who has been crying draws with his palm on each cheek. There weren't many of those hotels, three or four of them, and houses scattering away from them in no apparent order. Not a conducive place, you might say, for holidays, but isn't that the mystery, how people crowd in groups into the most unlikely places, just because of the habits of people before them? And it wasn't very large either, it would sustain one night at a stretch and even at that MacAllister would be huffing in the bars about just breaking even, about the venue being an act of duty, altruism, his cultural gift to southern Sligo rather than a commercial proposition. But even there we made history in our own small way because if the town could at the most sustain one performance we managed the quite extraordinary feat of playing twice on successive nights to what must have been to a man the same audience. By then, you see, Rene was far enough gone to have outgrown the first of our costumes, the one that was always used for the young, innocent parts, the Ophelias and Columbines. Most of her Rosalind was played in what you would now call drag—you do know the play—and for that she wore breeches and a smock that would have done for anything from The Saughran to Robin Hood. It was bulky, you see, hanging loose. But the scenes where she was Rosalind, the beginning and the end ones, she had outgrown the first dress and nobody had yet thought of the possibility of her changing into the more bulky, flowing, generally bald velvet or satin things that were pulled out for any part remotely middle-aged or regal. Our Gertrude dress, in a word. It seemed starkly obvious to us of course, her in that piece of cloth that was more like a nightdress than a theatrical costume. Her figure was adaptable though, and her movement seemed to melt her condition into herself, and needless to say knowledge of the fact of pregnancy leads one to see it in every gesture, but minus that knowledge one merely sees plumpness, roundness, or in her case, grace. But we had yet to be reassured by Rene in a larger dress and the pressure of her flesh on stage seemed to be caught everywhere in the lights, there was a desirability about her shape in that dress that was erotic, and so the fear and tension, the sense of urgency and secrecy, seemed to be rising on the stage like water. Or was it, I wonder, just her presence? She seemed to radiate desire and the pressure of eyes on her seemed to form a glow which made more people look in turn. But for me, I saw it as fear, fear simply of discovery, and the electricity of our combined emotions seemed to pull the play towards its end in one huge, erotic gasp. And again at the end we almost laughed with relief when the curtains went down and we heard, after a space, the sound of the clapping of hands.

'But that had been the pattern since Knock. The reason Strand Hill was so memorable, and I can see it now, is the small man with the neat white beard sitting on the veranda of the Strand Hotel. He came on the second day, was instantly recognised and instantly avoided. He was, you see, the drama critic of the *Irish Times*. His and our embarrassment were naturally extreme, since he was on what he hoped would be a quiet holiday and was obviously on quite friendly terms there with a Roscommon widow with whom he wouldn't be seen dead in Dublin. So company and critic passed one another in lounge and foyer and smiled gently as they did so as if to pretend the second-rate surroundings didn't exist, or if they did, only for the benefit and use of the other. But he must have attended on the second night because several days later we got some column-inch in the *Irish Times*. He mentioned Rene by name and what is worse traced her mother's acting history. The gist of it was, you see, that the west was somehow awake, that the dramatic genius of the first decade of the century was springing up a decade later, in the most unlikely of places—'

火

THE DUNES ARE reputed to be unusually high, almost curling round the nearest hotel to them, and when the drivers have unloaded their cars and Luke and Brogan have carried the properties inside they must all walk down by the dunes, past the dunes and find that their bulk has been obscuring a long sweep of beach. Despite the wind and spray there is something compelling about a long stretch of beach, like the suck and draw of the tide that hits its left side, and so they are drawn naturally into the wide sweep of empty sand, almost as

if they want to inhabit it, to mar its emptiness with their figures.
And the hallucinatory pull of empty sand increases if anything with
penetration of the beach, since there is always another stretch to be
walked across, quite virgin, with only the ridges where the sand has
gathered, driven by the wind. The brothers, standing hands on caps
by the open doors of their cars, can see them set out as quite a ho-
mogeneous group and as they walk down farther, scatter gradually,
like pebbles thrown across the white expanse by a hand, seen in slow
motion. Rene is somewhere in the centre of that group, becoming
a thin, almost single thread, only recognisable by the evenness of
her walk. And the crash and boom of the tide on the wet sand that
coats the air with its moisture. This is their first beach of that tour
of course, and the reason for their tour of course is summer and
beaches and so there they must feel that they have truly begun. That
the other beginnings were rehearsals for this one. The more experi-
enced ones of course, and Lili your experience with them then was
three years old, would know while they would lose sight of that sea
repeatedly through the rest of that summer, that sea would be their
only plumb-line. It would be to them the way it is to a car, along
a rocky coastline, where it disappears out of sight, is forgotten for
long stretches and is welcomed on reappearance, like an old friend
or an ultimate purpose. And they will leave it for nights, weekends,
even half-weeks, when the line runs more conveniently through an
inland town like Ballina. But there's a perpetual return when each
line reaches its end and there is the last small station, the structure
of which changes continually, and the colour of the platform and indeed the nature of the platform's adornment, and on leaving the station, there are the two hired cars to be taken to the view of beach and

sand and sea once more. And the older hands will take a knowing pleasure of course in recognising the drivers, in greeting them with the quiet familiarity and lack of ostentation that characterises such recurrent relationships. And all the drivers will wear hats since it was, apparently, what characterised the hired car then, in the absence of a sign, from the car owned privately. And the hats will perhaps remind Rene of the much too large and angular hat worn by that youth who waited so patiently on the Bray prom until her father told him, 'Home, Jack'. Though that first hat was military, but perhaps, like all first memories, the definition given to that hat was just like the definition given to first memories and she won't have noticed such a difference after all.

Lili, though, doesn't admit or recognise the importance of beaches, but looking at her in those breaks between her talking, I can see the memory of that series of beaches written on her face, on the threads of tiny veins across her cheeks, for all the world like the criss-cross of currents on an expanse of water seen from above and on the still fine, though parched and paper-like skin on her hands, like those dried husks of cod's roe one finds way beyond, generally, the sea's edge, transparent, that scrape gently when you touch them and that are of course covered with a fine sheen of sand, for all the world like the down of hair. Her bones now seem as delicate as those of a gull's skull, bleached, of course, and washed quite clean and when she opens her eyes to talk again they are bright, piercing and enthrallingly blue.

42

T HE WALK FROM the Bray station to the Main Street passes a bowling green, a sunken lawn below sea level. It is flooded today as James passes and the black curves of three bowls can be seen, aqueous and silent. The wind which whips the bay behind him leaves that water unruffled. They greet each other at the presbytery door, both exhausted by the other's absence. James moves into the curate's parlour with relief and the décor of the small living-room brings back his ponderous, dark gestures that were once framed on Tuesdays by his own bay window. The arguments begin at once of course, although instead of Luke there is an aged greying lady in a green apron, strangely male in her angular movements, to bring in the tray with tea. James eats the tomato sandwiches and notes with affection how the flesh around Father Beausang's collar has thickened. The excitement at their renewal of acquaintance, moderate at first, fills the room, then drifts and seems about to escape them, just to return, stronger than ever. Father Beausang's eyes light with enthusiasm as he elaborates a conceit of his own, a numeral system based on trinities. James's amazement is tempered by the curate's smile, coloured once again with his old, wayward humour. No, not on the Trinity itself, he murmurs, but on a triadic base, which gives quite different, exciting results than that of your binary code. Would a society, Father Beausang muses, whose mathematics were built on a triadic code, have radically different social characteristics? Two, after all, is an oddly unsatisfying concept. With two one has the dialogue, the linear, but with three one has the conspiracy of space. And thus the triangle, perhaps even more than the circle, is the symbol of harmony; of definition within unity rather than just unity itself. Of course such a triangle can admit of no intrusion. A new element added and it becomes a square, another and it becomes a pentagon—

Father Beausang stops and sees the world as a garden ravaged by intellect. James is staring into his cup. Father Beausang shifts forward and dust ruffles from his cassock, which blurs and haloes James's face. I kept this for you, Father Beausang whispers, I thought you would want to know. He extracts the faded cutting from the *Irish Times*. James takes the square of paper from his soft fingers, which seem reluctant to withdraw. Emerald at Strand Hill, he reads. MacAllister's Western Wonder.

⚸

THEY WALK TOGETHER past the bowling green and the submerged bowls and part at the station. The curate grips his elbow as the train draws in.

⚸

'YOU KNOW I never liked him. But perhaps that was jealousy. Or the impatience that uncertain people always rise in me. But then I loved Luke. They were so alike. Did I love him too? She did. And she loved me. When he came to that hotel in Gort and Luke saw him through the glass and ran to him, I hated him. I thought it was over. But I was wrong there too. I know that three of them were necessary. Now I know that. You ask me who was the father. I say both of them were. He had been following us, you see, from sometime back in Sligo. Some place, I mean,' she thought for a moment. 'And he found us in Gort. Or was it in Lisdoon?'

ᕱ

AS THE TRAIN pulls him with an ease that must have been like a long silk ribbon, since he is not conscious of stops, station changes or of the evolutions of landscape through the window, he remembers those bowls sitting on the grass, the slight upper curve above the quiet surface and the sphere below distended and enlarged by the water that held them in its pool of green. He realises that bowls seem always at rest, even when thrown, but he has never seen bowls so much at rest as these, the spaces across which they normally spin occupied by water. And the water touching each eliminated distance, and the need for movement. He reaches Ballisodare about midday and books one of the capped drivers to take him to Strand Hill. The other driver follows close, capped and curious, since James is the only passenger.

ᕱ

THE CAR WHEELS into the square of cement and comes to rest between the sea and hotels. They have left Strand Hill, of course. His conversation with the cloth-capped driver has told him as much.

James pays and walks across the square to the hotel that looms towards the sea and weeps its granite. The few posters in the lobby
tell him the same. He has forgotten the date, but no matter, those
posters hang limply from their corkboard with the sense of an event
that has passed. To where? he wonders. Another town, but which?
He sees her round, childlike signature in the guestbook and books
that room. It is a single room, he finds, with a bare, narrow bed. His
eyes crinkle in disappointment or affection, imagining Luke's bed
three rooms down from it. He sits on the bed and the boom of the
sea comes through the window like something solid and he regrets
for a moment the camera he has left swinging in Sydenham Villas.
The grey light of those western seaboards that seems more an echo, a
reflection of light than light itself, that vanquishes the space between
each stone, each hill, quickens his senses with the urge to capture it
once more, to photograph. But instead he sits there with, I imagine,
a growing sense of relief, drawing his eyes as near to the window as
possible, and all the scenes he has taken come back with the precision
of memory alone. They return fast as if pulled by the ribbon of those
years, each replaced by another, the moving picture of their souls.
He sees Luke age from puppy fat to sinew, he sees her move in three
large leaps to womanhood and it seems to him that the only sprocket
moving them is love. Their surfaces, as he views them, change and
shift and never settle, but it is light, he knows now, only light that allows him to view them and the light is that of love. And the light that
alone brings the booming sea outside to him floods through the glass,
filling the room with its weakened cobalt, a presence itself.

火

'YES, IT WAS Gort, Gort. We were in the lounge and he saw us through the glass, coming in. He must have travelled down the coast from Sligo. Difficult, I'd say, since the tour was out of rhythm. He must have gone to each town and asked. Then searched around for the next one. And asked again.'

⁂

HE READS THE provincial papers but finds no ads anticipating her, only reports in retrospect, after she has passed through. He walks out on to the cement square. He sees the long stretch of sand, virgin once more, and feels their presence somewhere down that coastline. The air is wet with spray, the clouds are full again and his quest is somehow fixed, that fullness drawing him on. He knows their absence is illusory. He asks the driver to take him to the train.

⁂

'THE MORE SHE grew, of course, the better he could find us. The fuss got bigger as she did, the crowds kept coming, larger each time. And the reviews. That article compounded it. The *Times* couldn't outdo the *Independent* or *Press*, I mean, and we soon had the problem of meeting all sorts of critics in the oddest places. The newspaper style then was the crushed cap and notepad and the chewed stub of pencil. You'd see them lounging in the back rows of those crowded halls, chewing and writing, chewing and writing. What was happening on the stage had almost ceased to be important. We changed the play, and they hardly noticed—'

⚹

IN BALLINA THERE is no beach, just the inlet of Killalla pointing
towards the heart of the town. He finds a poster, flapping on a
lamp post. He walks towards the hall in which the Emerald Theatre
Company played. The bowls move towards each other and click.
The front-of-house doors are arrayed with posters sagging from their
pins. He pushes the bar and walks through the door, as hesitant as
ever. It is a parish hall, with frames of de Valera and the Virgin on
the left-hand wall. There are rows of seats screwed to the floor which
give the hall some air of theatrical purpose. The open door throws
light towards the stage and a breeze must be sawing through for the
dust rises from the bare boards and wheels in circles and cones.

⚹

'SUMMER HAD COME. The heat grew and there was a stretch in the
days. Rene's Rosalind grew with the heat. We used the white gown
for her with oceans of room. We had to thread it with green. The
heat in the halls was cloying, but we bore it. We weaved onwards,
swelling as we went. MacAllister lost more of his hair—'

⚹

HE KNOWS THEY must travel by rail and that being the summer they
would favour resorts. He draws a rough itinerary of the seaboard
towns nearest the rail lines. He will look for signs, he thinks, that
will point the way forwards. These signs will be waiting for him,

to be teased out from the façades of towns, the surfaces of streets. In one square there is a Civil War statue with a stone cap staring beyond the roofs of houses. In another lies a cement road crumbling into beach and burrows. Modes of transport, he knows, can tell him a lot, the texture of each station his train pulls into and the car or buggy that draws him when his train fails. Hotels can tell him more, the shapes of window, bed and wash handbasin, the odour of boiled cabbage lingering in the hallways. There is no hurry, he knows, for once his journey is measured in minutes no longer but in a unit of time that has its own momentum, has no need for numbers. He senses that his looking for them is as vital as his finding. He swims at each beach he comes to and is hesitant entering each stage door. He questions young girls in hotel porches about everything but her and finds himself led back to her in the most delightful way. He talks of the weather, of the holiday season, of the big house. The wave that hits his body at each new beach seems a cousin of the last one. The posters pull him onwards with a rhythm of their own. Summer golfers tell him how the wind drives each ball eastwards, how one's best bet is to slice an angle towards the sea. Young maids have quite forgotten de Valera's sweep of here in 1919. The rocks his father painted begin to seep through the landscape. Schoolteachers tell him the history of each rath, each crumbling wall. Her posters vanish from one town and reappear in the next. Everyone is somehow related. He learns of her by proxy, in the most delightful way. She grows in the descriptions of her as he moves downwards, or is it that people raise their voices more? The rock comes to flood the landscape, pushing out the grass. He avoids large towns, since they never speak as much. The grass grows lusher, in green defiance, as

the rock encroaches. There is the plenty of the season and the vegetables crowd the shop-fronts and a vat of milk spills and floods a
broad street. He walks through it past a church entrance where the
milk laps the feet of the Virgin's statue. They multiply themselves as
he travels southwards and all roads lead to hallowed places, while
seeming to lead just to other roads. He searches them out in turn,
the trees copper with hammered pennies, the rivers flowing upwards,
the cloths that simulate blossoms on the blackthorn branches. There
are fields of rock now, intricate, ornate, more luxuriant than grass.
A nun talks of her in Spanish Point on a beach where the sea meets
a river. He finds she fills imaginations now and the white and pink
house fronts of Milltown Malbay are dotted with posters. An election coming, a capped man told him, driving through. And beside
hers, he sees, is one for de Valera. The posters thicken as he drives.
The rock, having ousted all grass, gives way to grass again. The posters flap in the east wind and draw him away from beaches and he
senses an end, or an arrival. He moves in a half-circle, skirting the
coast. Descriptions of her grow, become personal, people talk more
of her and less of those delightful incidentals such as weather. And
on the train to Gort when a woman, fluttering her eyelids in the
harsh sun of the seat opposite him, talks of a chance encounter with
her childhood friend, he realises what he knows now he has all along
known, that she is pregnant.

火

'AND THE LAST few towns were those little ones in Clare. It was all
her walk and her sense of poise could do to hide it, no matter what

clothes she wore. We circled round those towns as if MacAllister wanted to exhaust the whole of Clare. Lisdoonvarna was to be the end, you see, the festival week, you know about it, September in Lisdoon. So he pushed his time to the limit, dicing with fate. We tried to walk as little in public as we could, was it verging on the blasphemous, I wondered. We met some nuns in Spanish Point, like awkward birds they were, clutching their habits in case the wind clutched instead, and I could have sworn they guessed. But we made it to Gort, which was the last one before Lisdoon. We drove into Gort as the sun fell over the square. I know the sun never falls but it seemed to be then, just frozen in fall, lighting the bronze hair of that anonymous man of '98, was it, and the bronze shaft of his pike. We sat in the hotel lounge watching the light travel up to the tip of that pike as the sun went down. And it was that deflected, amber light full with the dust of late summer when I looked through the glass door out to the lobby and saw the front door open a little, then stop, as if outside someone had changed his mind. Was it a premonition or was it that I recognised his way of opening doors? I remembered that day in the advertising studio. I wasn't surprised when I saw him stooping through the doorway. Neither was Luke, who jumped up, opened the other glass door to meet him and said with a voice that could have included the whole world, Father, we are pregnant.'

SEVEN

LISDOONVARNA

43

THE GREAT SOUTHERN Railway looped a triangle then round the miraculous Burren. The main line ran from Galway southwards, through Gort and Ennis where a narrow-gauge single-track flowed off, like a seasonal tributary, towards Ennistymon, Inch and the beaches at Kilrush. The line of the coast completed the triad. And though the narrow-gauge is long out of use, as I travel with Lili on the broad one towards Gort I think of how the bare facts of landscape are softened by patterns like these. There are platforms of rock, bare scourings on the landscape, the remains of stone churches that have the grandeur of signs. There is map upon map, the excreta of years, harder now than the rock itself. So the Great Southern line followed the contours of a landscape which set the pattern of ages and the movements of people who were followed by MacAllister who was followed by Rene who was followed by James and is followed by me. De Valera sped behind them in a car, towards his election posters. Everything, James Vance learned when he entered that Gort hotel, belongs to everything else. Brigit, the *Vita Sanctorum* tells me, traced her own Clare itinerary, leaving meadows where bogs were. The train shuttles and pulls us forward, equipped with broad felt seats and neck rests and Formica tables in between. Lili is delighted by movement. She points to the sunlight, sheared by the procession of hills. Did you notice a car, I want to ask her, speeding past the tracks bearing a gaunt frame in a gabardine coat? But she doesn't hear. Who am I to question things? I wonder as the train pulls us through Ennis, past where the Kilrush summer track lies rusted and worm-eaten. I will follow James and alight at Gort and the texture of the platform will be a firm ageless blue-grey, the colour of those slabs that run from here, I'm told, to Moher, that raise their grassless, earthless shoulders somewhere to my right and slope down, all cracked sweeps and crevices, to the sea. Flowers of rare beauty bloom in those crevices. I rest content with imagining them, as I must with imagining that other, innocent, narrow-gauge track and the black and gold livery of the G.S.R. engine searing like a dash of Victorian optimism through that landscape of grey rock and green to the garland of towns by the sea.

The train gathers speed and Lili's delight grows. Somewhere to my right she gave birth to the child with two fathers, father and son themselves. History headed towards that fact and seems to end in me as great gusts of air begin to shoot through the carriage carrying the odour with them, is it of decay, of limestone, of diesel or generation? Lili has opened the window, I see, and the air rushes in. I breathe in more than I should. The draught hurtles through the window to the melodeon doorway and lifts the black veil off a nun in the seat beyond us, exposing a pair of grey fluttering lashes and eyes.

I stare at the sparse grass passing in the field beyond the bare whitethorn. It would have been the end of summer when James reached Gort and the whitethorn would have been just like that, bare since the spring, and he would have watched with me the grass slowly vanish, combed from the rock to leave it grey and formless, until the train slid between blocks, small ones first, then large enough to form a platform, and the train steams into that blue-grey texture, the steam and the rock surface both absorbing the light until all around the windows, through which James can see the town appear, is this metallic glare. The train stops then and the smell of diesel fills the carriage with the grey-blue light.

火

'Now who would have known,' said Lili, 'when he stooped in that doorway, and Jesus when I saw his stoop the sinking feeling came on me again—I mean, I knew the average door-jamb was too small for him but why couldn't he bend from the knees and make it a little less obvious, did generations of joiners and wainwrights, I mean, set about perfecting the average height of the Irish doorway just to give him an opportunity to stoop from the shoulders? But even given his permanent sense of apology to the world at large, who could have foreseen the odd marriage the three of them would make? Johnny Newham was at the bar and Ferdia O'Haodha and beyond them MacAllister and beyond him in turn me, in whom the old goat was at last taking some interest. But all three of us saw the door open a little and then close and then finally open fully and then this stooping shadow that we knew must have something to do with Luke—I mean, his length and his transparency were all there in embryo. Have you ever seen a plain mother whose features transpose themselves, item for item, to her daughter and emerge there incomparably more beautiful? Well this image of length and hesitancy that turned to beauty in his son got up to greet him and stood there, neither of them touching and yet both so much the image of the other's hesitation it was as if they were embracing. And Luke said "Father . . ." No, you couldn't have told seeing James Vance coming in the door what was to emerge. We had assumed Luke was the father. But seeing them beside one another you could sense it, scent it. The smell of that incongruous union filled the bar, I mean, like ripe apples or steaming hay—'

☆

WALKING OUT OF the limestone station a kind of fetid air like steam or hay did fill the streets. But then it had just rained and the last heat of the day was raising vapour from the pavements. There was the square, much as Lili described it, and not too far from the station either with a glorious stone pikeman the blue-grey of that whole county, the sun glancing the blade of his pike into fire. A cart loaded with September hay passed us and the scent of rotting stayed behind. Lili led me towards a plain hotel. The cart drove slowly round the pikeman to the westward road.

☆

IT IS WHAT all the surfaces intimated. The plate of dull metal, the sheen of blue, the shreds of eucalyptus rotting on the sloping hill. Everything turns into everything else, James realises, almost at the end of his passage through that country where everyone is related. Cousins once and twice removed, fathers, sisters, sons and brothers seem to await him in that bar which he fills now with his scent of damp hay, sweet, heady and glutinous. The scent of decay, he realises, is not far from the scent of birth. Nothing is separate.

※

THE LARGE WOODEN doors were open and led towards a foyer in which everything was wood. The jamb was low so that even I had to stoop to avoid cracking my forehead. Am I as tall, Lili? She doesn't answer, but walks briskly to the glass doors and pushes them open, squinting after the low sunlight outside.

※

'SO THOUGH I had almost willed,' she whispered, since the lounge before us seemed to impose silence, 'his head to crack on that jamb, when he came towards us with Luke, I couldn't. There were so many things I didn't know, I realised, and one of them was that between Luke's demeanour and his there was no difference, no difference at all. My sly passion for that whey-skinned youth, which was my passion for Rene, how could it not be my passion for the kid's father with whom for all I knew Rene was more passionate than with any of them? That was one of the things I didn't know. The other was that Rene was more pregnant than even I'd calculated. She always had an adaptable figure. Did I tell you that? And when they came towards me I couldn't care which of them was father. Which of them was Luke even. And MacAllister's beam was the largest of all. Well, I'm blessed! he said, when I told him who the tall one was. And when he was introduced, he said it again: Well, I'm blessed!'

※

I WALKED FROM the lounge through the wooden foyer. Lili stayed there, at the glass doors. The wooden front doors threw in an oblong cascade of light and framed the square outside, half amber sky, half blue-grey brick. The foyer narrowed and changed to a corridor which narrowed again. I knew now it was eternally simple. Each through loving each loves the other, father, son and her. Could I forget the perennial which, I wondered, hoping the rooms would provide an answer. But the wood of the corridor gave way to veneer and to a white tiled floor. I realised that I was in a recent extension, an architecture that could never have been fifty years old. So I walked back to the foyer and climbed an oaken staircase, certain that it would lead to the old rooms, so strong was the scent of generation from above. The oak curved under my hand as I went upwards and I was suddenly weak with pity for her, whom they both loved through each other. The scent grew as I ascended, and with it my pity. She had to bear all of them, I thought, as well as me. Two rows of doors stretched down the upstairs corridor. I chose one, following my nose. I edged the door open and saw white gauze curtains flapping by an open window. There was a table beneath it, with a curved jug and an oval hole which once would have held a basin. I went inside. There was a narrow bed. I stood for a while breathing the scent of clean linen. The scent changed then, as if a woman had entered behind me. I turned, but there was no one there. The room was as empty as ever. Then I saw the open window, where the exhaust from the Lisdoonvarna bus was drifting past. Nothing is distinguishable, I realised. The exhaust curled through the window like a beckoning finger. A wind brushed the curtains once more. I walked out then, down the stairs towards Lili and the waiting bus.

44

THE ROAD TWISTS and turns so much that our bus seems always to plough through the cloud of dust and diesel it has just
created. It is no coincidence that every bend is the bend we have just
turned and that but for the balding landscape our road would seem
almost circular, just as it is no coincidence that when Rene, James
and Luke ploughed through this road (and there was more dust
then) de Valera followed soon after with his driver, Jack. Neither is
it coincidence that what fields there were on either side were strewn
now, as then, with gouts of cut, yellowing hay. For all three trips
were made in September the way most trips to Lisdoonvarna are
and were, and the cut hay yellowed what fields there were round the
town where the unmarried gathered on verandas looking for spouses
and the feeble looking for cures. It seems more than the smell of
hay as we all drive forward, circuitously towards the town that I
have never seen, a recreative town, Lili tells me, without the sea.
But how can people holiday, I ask Lili, without beach, sea, promenade and Eagle's Nest? There were spa waters there, she told me,
which compensated. And that smell of hay which grows thicker as
we corkscrew forward as if we are piercing towards the generative
process itself reminds de Valera of nothing so much as the yellowing
water that comes from the round hole of the sulphur spring. He is

familiar with all the rites of his small nation. He has memorised the
precise balance of sulphur, iodine and phosphorous in the separate
springs and yet all four springs are one to him, part of that healing
process, the bubbling core, the well of cold health, Clare, renewal,
that elusive elixir of abstention politics and national health. Rene,
being driven also by a hatted driver in a car in which Lili took the
front seat with her and Luke and James the back, takes the smell
as the corollary to the colour of her hair and her condition. And
it was, Lili swears, as if it were made for her, a kind of supplicant
enticement, and every field we passed through bright only in so far
as its yellow gouts of hay matched the colour of her extraordinary
hair. I could feel her responding to it, her leg would tremble against
mine, or was it just the antics of that extraordinary driver? He remembered us from last year, you see, and even he had heard, knew
in advance, the reputation of our current tour and drove so the car
leapt over that road, seemed to rise from the tarmac when we took
those tangential bends and seemed to be driving round, back up our
own behinds, but with a speed and lightness that made it a journey,
a real journey. Her leg trembled and I drank in the smell of vegetation, cut vegetation, hay-sodden grass or falling leaves, I couldn't
have distinguished, but the kind of smell created by those years of
falling that made the boglands, didn't they, I could hear the crash-
ing of mile-high trees, evergreen leaves that you couldn't see now
and the vegetable matter pressed into earth, oil and peat-moss and
growing and falling again, and that this whole circus left just this
delicate film of hay on those stubbled fields seemed to me—well, a
final affirmation if you like, that brutal machine of years and that
yellow down which at times looked even more fragile than the flat,

even watery, texture of her hair. But that tremor—it runs from her thigh now down to her instep—it could have been—I had no idea, as I said, how advanced.

※

OUR BUS HEADS for a cloud of vapour that's like an embryo of the fields that generated it and passes through it, leaving its own cloud of dust and diesel. I can see the hay is falling off the fields now and the fingers of rock are showing through, a kind of crystal greyness that makes one think at first it is a trick of light, a refraction of the blue above.

We turned a corner, Lili tells me, or rather lurched round a corner, and she was thrown against me or rather sucked against me as if by a wind, and I was pressed in turn to the door. I could feel the pressure of something more than her body though, was it the heat or that cloying autumn smell, for a kind of September heat did fill the car along with everything else. But it was more than just heat, it was a pressure which could have been her weight, for as I told you her figure was adaptable and I had—we had—no idea of how far gone she was. But it was more than that too because for once James Vance seemed to sit upright behind me and had discarded his stoop and for once the driver's cap low down over his eyes didn't irritate me. It was—I hardly dare to say it, is there such a thing—the pressure of our happiness. Or hers. On me. Then the car lurched the other way and she fell away.

※

THE WINDOWS IN Dev's car are tight though as he is forced gently against the door and then forced away again with the car's movement. His face is abstract and expressionless, though somewhat kindly, eternally fixed in that gaze with which it met photographers, as if now it is anticipating a photograph. It never changes. The mouth is turned downwards without a hint of sourness, but in a contemplative moral curve, hardly departing from a straight line that is sad if anything, conscious of its need for consistency. His eyes are greyblue, echoing the rocks that are filling the fields now as the hay falls off and the strict, wire-rimmed glasses shine with a hint of that blue that is embedded in every transparency. His glasses are misting now with the vapour which, despite the closed windows, seems to seep through every crevice of the bodywork. Or is it just the heat he generates? Does his body steam with its own logic, embodying as it does generations of effort, the doctrines of eight centuries? This steam has the smell of hay, that musty, incongruously feminine smell as if, nourished on the peat of generations of the fallen, its inherited heat rubs, steams and oxidises. He is considering a scheme for turf-fuelled power stations. The steam on his glasses gathers, forms two separate tears which drop to his cheeks, as if his eyes had shed them. The car lurches once more and approaches the town.

火

WE TURN A last corner and travel upwards for a small hill, and the unmistakable sensation that we have arrived fills the bus. The air tells us, all of us, that we are here, where some moments ago we were not, though the bus is lurching one last time. The sense of water in the air

when the bus exhales to what is surely a halt in a small square ringed
with hotels led to by streets which are sprinkled with hotels as I help
Lili down. The bus coughs and moves on, leaves the square to the
two of us. But the porous quality of the air, the patient façades of the
hotels, every leaded pane of which seems to anticipate a sea where in
fact there is none. Where do these winds come from, I wonder, this
invisible vapour, that sense of mild bluster redolent of hay instead
of brine? Every house is an informant, every shop-front seems built
for a beach, and the gaunt metal frames yawning from each window,
some of which hold that loose striped canvas, seem to demand a
placid stretch of canvas deckchairs, their wooden struts sunk in the
yellow sand. Was there a sea here once, I wonder, that rolled back,
the texture of which this town wants to re-create, remembering an
impossible golden age? The hotels face each other in mute pathos,
the expectations of each belied by the others' presence, in mutual
pretence that the others aren't there. Which one did they stay in? I am
overcome by the multiplicity of choices and the porous air. All four
of us sit on the white metal seats.

火

WE WALKED TOWARDS a patch of green and a white metal seat.
There was a black, bowed figure on it. I recognised the folds of fat
round the neck and the collar flecked with dandruff. I tapped him on
the shoulder and raised a small cloud of dandruff like pollen from
heather. It was indeed Father Beausang. He rose and stretched his
hand towards Lili, his head bending forwards, a little too eagerly.
Forgive me for following, he whispered after I'd introduced them,

but I couldn't help myself. He squeezed my arm, as before. I took
Lili's, and we walked around the square.

火

I PICTURE HER wearing a bulky, shapeless fawn-coloured coat. They
all spill out from the cars into the empty square. She has her hands
in her pockets and so drags the coat downwards, pear-shaped from
her narrow shoulders. She loses James and then Luke walking past
the hotel fronts. They see her among the faces and lose her again.
She walks past the awnings and the leaded windows wondering will
one of these roads bring her to the sea that all the façades seem to
promise. She comes to the square and sees the grey shoulders of the
mountains beyond it. Luke quickens his step and comes up behind
her but then stops when his hand could touch her hair to call her
back. He lets her walk from him. There is a patina of dust in the air
and from somewhere the cries of children. A hotel door bangs. Every
shop is closed. She sits on the white metal seat. Jack swings the car
round one last corner and into the square. The proxy tears have va-
porised again on his master's cheeks as the car circles once round her
seat. There will be stuffed trout on the walls of his master's hotel and
a large plaster statue in all three bedrooms, grey walls that are saved
by the poignancy of the window's vista, the quiet graveness of this
square and the yellowing landscape broken only by the grey mound
of hills beyond. He will drive him to the spa under different condi-
tions than in 1919 and watch him drink his yellowed sulphur water
from the brass chained cup without any sense of urgency. Then drive
to Spanish Point, perhaps, Quilty, Milltown Malbay and beyond.

Each town square will have only the surprise of recognition for him, notable only in so far as it is so much the same. Before he hears the disyllable Home, Jack. He stops the car and helps his master out and they walk towards their chosen hotel.

۸

OLD AGE BRINGS a certain sweetness, said Father Beausang. What a pity James didn't experience it. I would get postcards from him from the places he went through. Knock, Strand Hill, Ballina, Quilty. I knew hardly any of them, Salthill was the West Coast to me, so you can imagine how they loomed in my imagination. Lisdoonvarna I pictured as a town of gazebos, white metal bandstands . . .

۸

IT WAS TO be the climax of the tour, said Lili, but I must admit I can still remember our sense of anti-climax when we drove in. Other towns had been bustling, crowds lining the seawalk and the posters flapping for two weeks beforehand. Well the posters were here all right, but no crowds. Morris Minors lining the outsides of every hotel all right, but to all outward appearances, a sleepy inland town. That was what threw us, you see, the fact that it was inland. I had to remember all over again. These aren't seaside hotels, I had to remind myself, though they looked like it. These are spa hotels. So we pulled up and opened the doors and that heady vegetable scent of fullness exhaled and seemed to fill the streets. I could almost see it, like the yellow dust that rises with haymaking, drifting towards each open window saying,

We are here. That it would get to them I had no doubt, on reflection. I
had to remember, you see, that here it all happens indoors.

⚹

WE CROSS THE square towards the spa road. Dev strides ahead and
Jack follows behind. They talk mathematics as they walk, a mutual
love, even a necessity for all his personal staff. Jack's uniform becomes lined with sweat, inevitably; there is not a breath of wind and
the green texture of his Free State jacket loses any semblance of fresh-
ness, that bright sycamore green conceived in the childhood of this
state saturated with both dust and moisture seems aeons old now,
dandruff-flecked as if seeking out and exhaling in its turn the odour
of years of vegetation, falling, regeneration and decay. They discuss
the combustible potential of peat turf in kilowatts, ohms and ergs.
The miracles wrought by the historical Brigit occur to him, who created flames out of mud and sand in an empty grate, who transformed
an arid bog into a field of yellowing hay. He makes a mental note
to visit her well, Liscannor, on the heights beside Moher. He passes
Rene who must have seemed the embodiment of this yellow, but of
course he doesn't notice since his sight, bad at the best of times, has
become clouded with her vapour, condensing into tears again on his
rimless glasses.

⚹

THE ROAD CURVES from the town and the hotels fall away to be
replaced by the borders of nodding fuschia. The scent is musk and

heady and there's the hum of wasps. Your first impact with Lisdoon, Lili told me, is deceptive for it is only when you have entered your hotel, signed the guestbook and settled down in some lounge for an afternoon snifter you realise the secret life of the place. Those bent shoulders in those wood-panelled snugs don't belong, as you might think, to the usual assortment of cattle-jobbers and afternoon chemists but to bachelors in search of unwed ladies, matchmakers, fathers, uncles, cousins once removed, all treating with beautifully embarrassed civility subjects of the utmost delicacy. There's no spitting on hands and hearty jokes. Instead there are everywhere deep blushes and sweating necks under stiff collars and stifling Sunday suits. Which might account for the extraordinary humidity of the place which I noticed had grown ever since we left Gort and went round and round those yellow September fields, but which once I entered the lounge of the Spa Hotel I found what possibly might be an explanation. Ah, I thought, it's the odour of embarrassment, the sweating pores of the rite known as courting, that vaporous sign emanating from the shy and gentle rural males of the snugs and lounges towards the spotless matron who sipped tea as a rule on the sun verandas facing the street. And morning and afternoon were just a preparation for night, during which the embarrassment and humidity reached their climax in foxtrots, quicksteps, halting conversations and even hurried kisses, in the midst of whatever entertainment the town could provide. It was with some trepidation that I realised then that we were to be the entertainment for the night, we were to provide the focus for this coughing, underspoken rite and MacAllister beside me, hands shaking as he poured his mixer into his gin, I could see he realised it too. Our last night, he said to the assembled company, and then—Dublin. Would Dublin be able to hold us though, I wondered, seeing the clouds of expectation gathered round the bar and the air settling in the street outside, the opaque texture of which might, I imagined, have originated from the spa and the sulphur springs.

文

DEV WALKS TOWARDS the spa with both fists clasped tight and his thumbs rigid, a brisk walk, his long frame upright and his profile etched against the afternoon haze, tilted slightly upwards, looking forward. The line of his nose, strong and almost elegant, is what seems to pull his body forward, echoed by two deep lines falling downwards to the curve of each lip. Were there ever lines deeper than those and is it the sense of smell that pulls him forward with the profile of his nose, towards some distant future? There is something military in his clasped fists, more than military even, since his pace is easier than that of Jack who is now quite drenched in sweat and the former bright green of his uniform is stained to what is more like an earth-coloured muddy brown. Used to cars, armoured carriers and even horses, this soldier is quite unused to walking and feels himself slipping into the mists of his own perspiration, can hardly find the will to keep his eyes raised to the rapid, easy feet of his chief, whose light step straddles the past and whose profile points towards any number of possible futures. The road curves and leaves houses altogether for a moment, then rises a little and falls again and Dev can see the fields with their splashes of yellow in the distance and the circular road through which we all have come and below him, on this road, the chalet which houses the spa. I slow my pace coming down towards it. Built of wood and raised on stilts, it is striped like a boating hat, rich cream and black, and between the stilts which raise the chalet like wary legs afraid of dampening the hem of a fine striped skirt there runs a river. A house over water. I think of how apt those hotels are with their beach-like fronts. But Dev is familiar, he is familiar with everything and he walks through the gates, down the avenue without losing a step.

·к·

LUKE, LILI TELLS me, despite the day's heat and excitement, had the sets up an hour early. Bless that boy, MacAllister said, and dragged us down an hour early to rehearse. We had come to the end, we knew, of Rene's costumes and I had managed to pucker the last one, her matron's smock, into something like a gown. The hall was wedged between decrepit hotels, and there was Luke when we entered illuminated by that cloud of smoke in the yellow footlights brushing down his canvas pillars, forests and his palace façades. We went through the scenes like sleepwalkers, the lines had so gripped us through repetition that they seemed not to exist anymore, what emerged was simply speech, undefined by words. How doth, sweet coz, said Rene and I saw how well my puckering had done its job; her figure, as adaptable as ever floated from shape to shape, caught by one footlight then by the next, and was like the words, indefinable. There was yellow gel over the footlights which gave her that ripened look. But this is September, I said when MacAllister wanted to change them, and yellow's right surely, and would you believe, I turned to James Vance for confirmation. I had forgotten his stoop, his apologetics, all my irascibility. We are all persons, I simply thought, or even person. Isn't yellow right, James? I called down into the belly of the hall but he wasn't there. I turned to Rene and would have pinched her cheeks to highlight the yellow but she wasn't there either.

☼

THE ROOF IS triangular. The water surges through the stilts and disappears. Then night was coming, says Lili. Amorous night. The humidity gathered and the chaff and the yellow had compounded the dark. It was a smell, that night, not a colour. All the sideways glances and the shy gazes and the throaty whispers. I was sent to find her. I found her down here by the pools.

☼

WE WALK DOWN long halls beyond the depths of the chalet and doors lead on either side to the pools, the brass taps. The sound of dripping seems everywhere, or is it Dev's footsteps echoed by those of Jack, or James's memories, perhaps each one dripping into that pool, which now envelop everything? The yellow sulphur water he drinks from the brass cup smells almost resinous and the elegant curves which the waters make from the flowing taps streak themselves with yellow and cream like his eucalypti of years ago. Everything turns to everything else, he thinks, and every image he has slid from his acid bath reappears in the damp oozing from the limestone and the encrusted brass of the tap handles. I see those pools leading to the caverns below and the large sea and every image this town implies reproduced in that darkness which intimates every form.

⚶

FATHER BEAUSANG BROUGHT a cup to his ageing lips. The messages were cryptic, he said. But how they spoke to me. I thought of James, his need for words diminishing. Of the talks we could have had. I pursued my researches into that exquisite system. Logos, the Word made Flesh, the aural connotations of the Virgin Birth. I made notes, hoping for lengthy discussions on his return.

⚶

DE VALERA COMES to the sister pools. He compares the motive powers of water with the combustible powers of turf. He lowers his lips to one, then the other. He sees his own face reflected, his spectacles like pools themselves. The curve of his mouth loses its strictness in the water's ripple. He sucks with extraordinary power.

45

W E WALKED BACK the long road from the spa to the square
of hotels. The light was fading and from the hedges the
fuschias gave their last musky exhalation. I walked between her and
Father Beausang through the scent on each side until the bushes gave
way to the first few houses and the hotels began. Night was then
down, amorous night. All the coloured bulbs swinging from the rooftops now came into their own. They glowed against the dark blue sky
and obscured the stars. They caught the bare outline of the fingers of
rock behind. They swung back and forwards, faintly moving orange
shadows across us as if in time to the thin music that came from
some hotel ballroom. Lili led us across the square to the hall of the
last performance and the lilt grew louder. There was a small queue of
people waiting to get in.

火

Do I HAVE to tell you, she said, how packed it was? You could hear
the silence and the held breaths and the close stiff bodies. The lights
in the house went down. The curtain came back and the amber lights
came up. Rene began her Rosalind. She said each line with an extreme quietude as if the time were there just for her. She moved from

left to right in a series of still poses that were hardly movement at all. We were terrified, offstage and on. How could they not notice—

✳

I PAID FOR all three of us and we walked inside. There was a shabby corridor with a lady taking coats. I gave her Lili's coat and got a ticket for it. Father Beausang kept his dark jacket. We walked towards the hall and the music got louder. I recognised the tune. Do you know it? I asked Father Beausang. He squeezed my elbow and whispered, the Anniversary Waltz.

✳

NEED I TELL you, said Lili, that they didn't notice? They became one single eye, staring. I saw Luke behind the flat with the ducal pillars. He was reaching forward through the darkness as if always on the point of walking on stage. I saw James on the other side. He had to stoop to keep his head below the canvas. I could see the smoke of MacAllister's cigarettes. I kept thinking of the end and the nuptial dance. I was waiting for it to come and hoping it wouldn't come. It was all a dance.

✳

WE WALKED THROUGH a pair of swing doors and the hall spread out before us. There was a band on the stage playing the chorus of the Anniversary Waltz. Couples swept in stiff and formal quarter-circles round the floor, mainly in one direction. They wore dark suits and white collars, navy skirts and patterned blouses, orange flowers on some bosoms, grey threads in hair. Some danced, some stood around the walls. The bachelors who stood around the walls waited for the dance to end. I excused myself from Father Beausang, took Lili in my arms and swept her out on the floor. Her hand clutched mine with a thin, brittle strength and the fluidity of her steps far outdid me. I trod on her toes. I apologised. My generation, I told her, has forgotten so much.

꙳

WE WERE QUITE bare, you see, on that stage. But there was a magic up here that disguised us. Her figure, as adaptable as always. Who would have known? I can remember a murmur down the hall then.

꙳

FATHER BEAUSANG SWEPT by me with a woman in blue. His small legs in their dark creases stretched upwards to accommodate her height. He was sharing some joke with her. She laughed out loud as she danced. He looked years younger, his face near hers.

꙳

I WAS AFRAID of that murmur. But it was just de Valera, I found out later. He came in late, with his driver chap.

꙳

LILI'S FACE WITH its multitude of creases and its fine down of hair. It was close to mine, her eyes were closed and her mouth had that smile of neither laughter nor pleasure but of remembered things.

You bring me back, she whispered. He was so like you.

Which of them? I asked her.

Both, she said.

I swept her up a small incline and on to the stage. The band were surprised but they kept on playing. The Emerald Ceilidh Band, said the lettering on the bass drum. We danced up there, while the hall danced below. The rhythm was 3/4, simple, eternal.

⚔

SO HE CAME in, said Lili, the father of us all. I didn't see him. He took his seat like the rest of them. We waltzed towards the end.

⚔

THERE WERE SHREDS of curtain obscuring a proscenium arch. The footlights were weak, glinting in the metal of the organ and the electric guitar. I swept Lili past the band into the comparative darkness backstage.

⚔

THEN THERE WAS applause. Quite a wind of it. Huge gusts of it, shudders. It pulled her dress against her. It must have been a wind.

⁂

THERE WERE TATTERED flats of a landscape of hills, of a blue sky, a tree. I saw the white flash of what could have been a pillar. We danced between them, stepping wide of the canvas flats.

⁂

SHE BOWED. FROM the waist, like a clown or a girl.

⁂

I DANCED LILI out into the lights again and down on to the floor. I swept her in the longest of arcs towards Father Beausang and left her in his arms. They danced together, which was, I suspected, what they both wanted. I stood there while the couples swayed around me. I would have waved my arms, I would have orchestrated all their movements but they were all beyond me now, moving of their own accord. And it was a ladies' choice, I discovered, when a youngish woman in a tight dress said to my face: Shall we dance?

46

W E TOOK THE Ennistymon road the next day in a hired car. Lili dozed on Father Beausang's arm. His suit was crumpled and his eyes had a slow, meditative look. Tell me about Woman, I asked him. He smiled softly. Think of generation, he said, conception and birth in its scriptural shape. How man was made in God's likeness and was given by woman to eat and how paradise died and the eternal now and how man became subject to chance, accident and time. But it was man who had eaten and woman who had given, man who engendered the seed of time and woman who nurtured it. Down to Joseph, he says, down to Mary and I can see that same haze touched with ochre and the almighty sun over some Judaean field and the oozing humidity of laurel groves. And woman therefore, says Father Beausang, loved by more than man, could not but give birth to the love-child untouched by time, resplendent, immortal. I see his eyes through the rearview mirror, shining softly. Lili shifts in the crook of his arm. We travelled, says Lili, back the roads we had come the next day, a sentimental tour you might say, but she wanted to see those trains again and we hired, would you believe, a separate carriage to take the whole company on the loop around the coast. Rene's love for trains had affected all of us and out we journeyed for all the world like children with packed lunches and picnic baskets. Did it remind her and Luke and James, I wondered, of their beloved Bray express, could that account for the bliss that filled the carriage once the old porter had slammed the door in Ennistymon and the train moved forward in bumps, each one of which bumped her between them. It was our last day of course, and which of them I could call father I cannot even now fathom, both of them or neither. Her happiness rippled through the carriage and illuminated each of the seats the dust rising off the red felt covers as it was beaten out periodically by our laughing backs. And what, I ask Father Beausang, of woman now? Now as always and his words seem slurred, awaiting the second coming. Can God come twice? I ask and as the road whorls and whorls and we plough through our own clouds he gives me an inventory of signs presaging that event. Son will not know father, he tells me, and minor rail tracks will fall into disuse. Photographic images will substitute for faces, colours will reach us with the texture of smells, everything will become everything else. Jack drives de Valera towards St Brigit's Well, Liscannor, and he stands on the heights and sees the historical Clare below him and points out the lands of Turlough the Packer O'Brien who could trace his lineage to Brian, to Niall, to Moses, to Adam and thence to God. Christ O my white sun, he murmurs and blesses himself passing the four crutches, entering the grotto, surveying layer upon layer of postcards, pleas and litanies fixed to the dripping stone. Who have recourse to Thee, he reads on the first one, Mother Immaculate he reads on the one below it. He peels away year after year until the dates and pleas become illegible, the faces of the Virgins fall away at his touch and he reaches the damp surfaces, whitened by mildewed paper, of the sodden rock where the water seeps through, beyond the reach of dates and years. The moisture clouds his glasses once more and promises tears. Home, Jack, he says. Could he be called a love-child? asks Lili, shifting in the crook of her prophet's arm. Father Beausang smiles. Her happiness flowed outwards in waves, she says, in shudders that ran through the whole carriage, rattling the picnic baskets. Was it her I wondered or the small twin-cylindered engine puffing out its gouts of steam below us that seemed to answer to every ripple of hers. And MacAllister was staring with his cheek to the window blissfully waiting for the first view of ocean when I felt the water lapping round my feet, up to my ankles then over my knees, and that smell, was it hay or years or just the steam outside, and it was going through a small rocky field, I remember, coming to a level crossing that I realised the water was real, not just her happiness and I pulled the cord. Jack cruises to a halt and beeps his horn at the standing train but Dev patient as ever walks from the car through the field to the aqueous window. Father Beausang tips Lili's cheek and now I in that standing train the steam of which was hissing towards silence through those waters and that musk of generation came.

NEIL JORDAN

NEIL JORDAN WAS born in 1950 in Sligo. He is the author of several critically-acclaimed novels including *Mistaken*, *The Dream of a Beast*, *Sunrise with Sea Monster*, *Shade*, and *Night in Tunisia*, a collection of short stories which won the Guardian Fiction Prize. He has written, directed, and produced a large number of award-winning films including *The Crying Game*, *Michael Collins*, *Interview with the Vampire*, *The End of the Affair*, and *Ondine*. He is currently the Creator and Executive Producer of the Showtime series *The Borgias*. He lives in Dublin.